Abigail Adams

Lady Phillips

Patr...

...ns

| DATE DUE | | |
|---|---|---|
| ~~FEB 1 5 2007~~ | | |
| ~~APR 1 4 2007~~ | ~~JAN 1 9 2008~~ | |
| ~~AUG 1 0 2009~~ | ~~APR 1 0 2009~~ | |
| ~~MAR 2 6 2011~~ | ~~JAN 1 4 2013~~ | |
| | | |
| | | |
| | | |
| | | |
| | | |

Phillis Whe...

...ine

# Justice for All

December 5, 1773 - September 5, 1774

By Amanda Stephens
Illustrated by the Flying Carnies

Grosset & Dunlap • New York

9 -03
7. 00

Liberty's Kids ™ and © 2003 DIC Entertainment Corporation
Published by Grosset & Dunlap, a division of Penguin Young Readers Group,
345 Hudson Street, New York, NY 10014.
GROSSET & DUNLAP is a trademark of Penguin Group (USA) Inc. Published simultaneously
in Canada. Printed in the U.S.A.
The 'See it on PBS KIDS' logo is a trademark of the
Public Broadcasting Service and is used with permission.

*Library of Congress Cataloging-in-Publication Data*
Stephens, Amanda.
Justice for all / by Amanda Stephens ; illustrated by the Flying Carnies.
p. cm. -- (Liberty's kids ; 1)
Summary: Boston in 1773 is an inhospitable place for the two teenagers
whose lives are about to intersect there.
1. Boston (Mass.)--History--Colonial period, ca. 1600-1775--Juvenile
fiction. [1. Boston (Mass.)--History--Colonial period, ca.
1600-1775--Fiction. 2. Boston Tea Party, 1773--Fiction. 3. African
Americans--Fiction.] I. Flying Carnies. II. Title. III. Series.
PZ7.S8315Ju 2003
[Fic]--dc21
2003005210

ISBN 0-448-43248-X          A B C D E F G H I J

# ☆ The Thirteen Colonies ☆

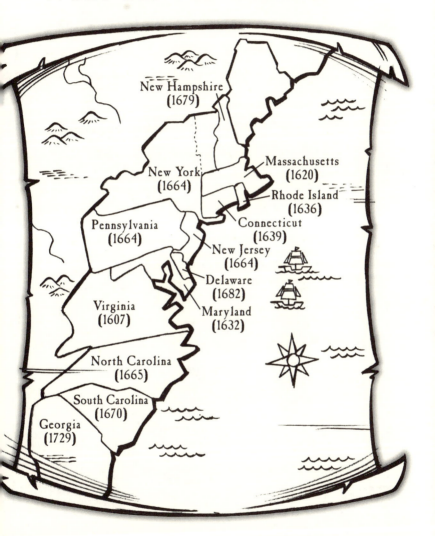

New Hampshire
(1679)

New York
(1664)

Massachusetts
(1620)

Rhode Island
(1636)

Connecticut
(1639)

Pennsylvania
(1664)

New Jersey
(1664)

Delaware
(1682)

Virginia
(1607)

Maryland
(1632)

North Carolina
(1665)

South Carolina
(1670)

Georgia
(1729)

5, December, 1773

Dearest Mother,

I can hardly believe it's been a fortnight since I bade you all farewell. I miss you terribly, yet, my heart is also filled with delicious anticipation of the new life that awaits Father and me in the colonies!

I look forward to settling in Dr. Franklin's home in Philadelphia. And I long to see Father again, when he returns from the wilderness.

The sailors tell me the colonies are a primitive place. I hope I'll grow to love it as much as Father does!

I wear his locket, always. I'm proud to have a brave explorer as my dad. We'll be reunited on the wonderful land he is sure to discover.

I shall be true to my word and write every day.

Your loving daughter,
Sarah

# ✫  ✫  ✫
# Chapter One
## ✫  ✫  ✫

Sarah Phillips sat in the small cabin below the deck of the sailing ship and placed her quill pen back in the inkwell. She looked at the letter she'd just written to her mother, who was still at home in England. The handwriting was a bit shaky, but that was understandable, considering the storm they were now sailing through. The wind above was horrible, and every now and then a crash of thunder would penetrate the monotonous silence in the ship's hold.

The Atlantic Ocean never provided an easy crossing; Sarah had been warned about that. But this storm was one of the worst the crew of the *Dartmouth* had experienced in a long time. And

*The Dartmouth*

Sarah was caught in the middle of it.

*Whoosh!* Sarah braced herself against the small plank table as the bow of the ship crashed down under an enormous swell of water. She swallowed hard. Her stomach was queasy. She wasn't seasick exactly, but food was definitely not something she would welcome.

Sarah sighed. She had hoped that by now, she'd have gotten her sea legs. She'd been sailing on the *Dartmouth* for days, cramped up in the little cabin, surrounded by crates of tea that were being shipped to the colonies.

The *Dartmouth* was basically a cargo ship, but it also served as a transport for a few wealthy passengers like Sarah, who were heading to the colonies from England. Making the journey on the *Dartmouth* wouldn't have been so bad had the weather been more cooperative. At least then the bright-eyed redhead could have spent some time on deck. But being stuck inside, breathing damp musty air, and trying not to think about the rats that scratched at the walls and the floorboards was a lot for this fifteen-year-old to handle.

The voyage felt endless. Sarah couldn't wait to put her feet on solid ground again. It would be nice to sit by the fire at the home of her mother's dear friend Benjamin Franklin. That was where Sarah would be staying until her father could come and get her.

That was a day that couldn't come soon enough for Sarah. Her father had been gone for so long. He was on a special mission for His Majesty, King George III of England. The king wanted to develop new colonies, in the wilderness west of the thirteen original colonies. Sarah's father, Major Phillips, was sent by the king to explore, and he was now somewhere far off in the Ohios. Nobody knew for sure what people lived in the Ohios—they could be friend or foe. There was no telling, until the British met up with them.

But Major Phillips was a brave man, and he'd been excited when he was called to duty. He had no fear of the new world he would be exploring . . . the world beyond the colonies. Sarah knew that no matter how primitive Philadelphia might seem compared with London, it was far more sophisticated than the land her father was now trekking across. She reached up for the gold locket she wore on a chain around her neck. It had been a gift from her father. Just touching the glimmering piece of jewelry made her feel braver.

*Crash!* A huge clap of thunder bellowed up above as the ship swayed back and forth under the weight of the mighty waves. Sarah's inkwell slid from the table and fell to the floor, smashing into pieces. A drip of ink splashed up, hitting Sarah squarely on the nose. As she wiped the dark black ink from her face, Sarah Phillips's eyes filled with fear.

Like her father, Sarah loved adventure. But this was more of an adventure than she'd ever bargained for.

# Chapter Two

Sarah Phillips wasn't the only fifteen-year-old having a difficult time that morning. As Sarah sailed across stormy seas, James Hiller, an apprentice in Benjamin Franklin's print shop, was facing a challenge of his own.

"Moses! Moses! Help!" James cried out as he yanked at his shirt. Somehow, the publishing apprentice had managed to get his shirttail caught in the printing press. He struggled to free himself. But the more he pulled on his shirt, the tighter the press's grip on the cloth became. "Moses! Hurry!"

A tall African-American man rushed into the print

shop. He stopped in his tracks when he discovered just what the emergency was all about. A slightly amused smile crossed his face. "Not again, James," he said, and sighed as he moved closer to the lanky, blond-haired teen.

"'Fraid so, Moses." James blushed with embarrassment. Not that Moses could tell—James's face was so covered with printer's ink that the pink in his cheeks could barely be seen. "Help me. This is my last clean shirt."

Moses pulled a lever on the printing press. Instantly, James's shirt popped free from the machine's grasp. "Thank you," James said.

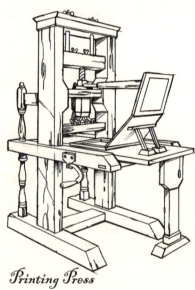

*Printing Press*

"Dr. Franklin warned you about standing too close to the press while it's printing. Look at yourself."

James turned and looked at the mirror behind Moses's shoulder. The front page of *The Pennsylvania Gazette* was printed across the back of his shirt. But instead of being upset by the idea of being a walking newspaper, James was thrilled. "Fantastic!" he exclaimed, grinning broadly. "I'll wear this on the street when I sell papers. It pays to advertise."

Moses shook his head. "We're paid to print the paper, not wear it."

James stood tall. "I don't just *print* the paper," he told Moses proudly, "I'm a reporter."

"You're an *apprentice* reporter," Moses said.
"True," James admitted reluctantly. "But someday I'm going to get the Big Story! Then Dr. Franklin will make me a full-fledged journalist."

Before Moses could remind James that until that time the paper still needed to be printed, an eight-year-old street boy with bright eyes and unruly brown hair came racing into the print shop, holding a letter in his hand. "It's from Dr. Franklin in London," Henri Lefebvre shouted excitedly in his French accent.

"Give me that, Henri," James said, reaching for the envelope.

Henri pulled the letter from the bigger boy's grasp. "It's addressed to Moses. Is your name Moses?"

"Your name is mud," James muttered to Henri as the boys watched Moses open the mail.

Unlike many of his fellow African Americans, who

were living as slaves and not taught to read, Moses was a free man who had learned to both read and write. Quickly, Moses scanned the note from Dr. Franklin. A look of excitement came over his face. "Lads! Drop everything," he announced. "Sarah Phillips isn't coming to Philadelphia."

"Good," James said matter-of-factly. "I never understood why she had to stay here, anyway."

"Fetch your coats, we're going to meet her at the ship," Moses continued, ignoring James.

"I thought you said she *isn't* coming to Philadelphia," James said, confused.

Moses held up the letter. "She's not. Dr. Franklin says Miss Sarah couldn't make passage on the *Dover*. She's aboard the *Dartmouth*, and the *Dartmouth* is heading for Boston."

James's eyes grew large. "Boston? That's in Massachusetts colony."

A look of concern came over Moses's face. He'd heard rumblings recently of conflicts in the Massachusetts colony. The people there were angry about taxes imposed on them by King George and Parliament. There was talk of rebellion. Boston was no place for a fifteen-year-old girl.

Moses grabbed the boys by the shoulders and

practically pushed them out the door into the snowy Philadelphia morning. "We have to hurry. She's all alone. Come on!"

✯ ✯ ✯

Moses wasn't the only one who feared for Sarah's safety during her long journey to the colonies. Her mother also was concerned—although she was grateful that her dear friend Dr. Franklin would be making sure Sarah was well cared for once she arrived in Philadelphia.

At the moment, Dr. Franklin was in London, on official business in his role as the Royal Postmaster for Pennsylvania. But he had complete faith that in his absence, Moses, James, and Henri would have no trouble keeping Sarah company in Philadelphia. And that's exactly what he told Sarah's mother, Lady Sarah Phillips, during a carriage ride through the streets of London on a cold and gray afternoon.

"I hope I'm not putting you out of your way, Dr. Franklin," Lady Phillips told her old friend as the carriage clacked its way over the cobblestone streets. She'd asked Mr. Franklin to come for a ride with her, just to help relieve her worries about her daughter.

"Not at all, Lady Phillips," he assured her as he adjusted his beaver skin hat. "I have an appointment just down the street. Besides, life's a wilderness without friends."

Lady Phillips sighed deeply and shut her eyes for a moment. "Last night I had a terrible dream," she confided. "My Sarah was in danger."

Benjamin Franklin smiled confidently. "Danger? In Philadelphia? Let me put your mind at ease. It's a fine city. The second largest in the empire," he boasted. "She'll feel very much at home."

"That is a relief," Lady Phillips agreed. She smiled briefly, but her face soon fell again. "I worry about her, Ben. With Major Phillips off scouting new land in the Ohios, Sarah will be all alone."

Ben Franklin reached over and gently patted Lady Phillips on the knee. "She won't be alone," he assured her. "She'll be in fine company with my associates, Moses, James, and Henri. Sarah couldn't be safer if she were still cradled in your own arms."

Lady Phillips smiled weakly at Ben Franklin and took his hand gratefully in hers. He seemed so sure that everything was going to be fine. Still, Lady Phillips couldn't shake the fear that something was going to go horribly wrong in the colonies.

# Chapter Three

Sarah stood on the stern of the *Dartmouth* and looked out into the night. The ship had only just sailed into Boston Harbor, and Sarah was anxious to get a glimpse of the city.

At first glance, the city seemed calm and quiet. But looks could be deceiving. In reality, there was trouble brewing in Boston. And within a few minutes of docking, Sarah realized that that trouble was aimed for the very ship she was on.

Sarah heard a man's deep voice ring out in the air like crackling fire. "The *Dartmouth*, let's burn it!" His cry was followed by shouts of agreement.

It was December 16, and a cold wind whipped at Sarah's hair, and nipped at her nose. But now Sarah was too frightened to feel the cold. The man's voice had been so menacing. It didn't sound as if he was making an idle threat.

Welcome to America, she thought as she reached up and fiddled nervously with her locket.

*** *** ***

Moses, James, and Henri weren't finding Boston any more hospitable than Sarah did. At that very moment, they were clicking and clacking their way over the cobblestone streets of Boston. They were dirty and tired from their long trip. As they looked around, they were disappointed in the city they'd arrived in. It didn't seem as sophisticated as Philadelphia. And the roads were certainly not as well paved. Their sore bottoms were proof of that.

"So this is Boston," James remarked, unimpressed. "It's smaller than I thought."

"My joints are aching from these rotten roads," Henri moaned.

Moses gave him an encouraging smile. "The axle is bent. It'll have to be repaired before we head back. The ride home will be smoother."

"Good," Henri replied.

The city of Boston might have been small compared with Philadelphia, but that didn't make it any easier to navigate. In fact, from James's point of view, the crooked, narrow streets that lay before them looked like a cramped, ominous maze. "How are we going to find Sarah?" he wondered aloud. "We don't even know what she looks like."

Moses thought for a moment. "She sailed on the *Dartmouth*," he suggested. "That's a good place to start." He shook the horse's reins, and the chariot set off toward the harbor.

As he led the boys through the streets of Boston, Moses felt there was danger in the air. It would be best to get Sarah Phillips and leave the Massachusetts colony as quickly as possible.

But they had to find her first.

★ ★ ★

Moses was right, there *was* trouble brewing in Boston. You could see it in the eyes of the colonists every time they had to pay a tax on their sugar or their tea. You could hear their frustration in the cries of the angry mobs that gathered each night.

Tonight, a group of colonists had gathered in a small tavern. The men were hoping to hear Sam Adams, a well-known revolutionary, give them the signal they'd been waiting for.

"Gentlemen of Boston! The hour has arrived!"

The crowd of men cheered wildly.

Samuel Adams did not smile. "Gentlemen, you know me as Sam Adams, neighbor and friend," he told them. "Hear me now! Parliament continues to treat us with ill will. First, the Sugar Act raised our taxes. Did we have a say? The answer is nay."

The mob of angry colonists booed and hissed. Sam Adams nodded in agreement and pulled a piece of paper from his coat. "Then the horrid Stamp Act nearly drove us to ruin," he declared.

The colonists knew all about the Stamp Act. No one in the colonies had been able to avoid it. The Stamp Act stated that colonists were required to buy a British stamp for every piece of printed paper they used. Every newspaper, document, and even playing cards were subject to this stamp tax. It was infuriating—especially because people in Britain didn't have to purchase stamps for their paper goods.

"And who can forget our brothers, who lost their lives in the Boston Massacre?" Sam Adams continued.

Now the crowd was going wild. They all remembered the Boston Massacre. It had taken place just three years before, during a scuffle between soldiers and colonists at the Boston Custom House. Five Americans had died, and seven more were injured.

*Sam Adams addresses the crowd.*

Sam Adams looked out over the crowd. The men were fired up now, angry, and eager to avenge the wrongs that had been done in Boston. "Now Governor Hutchinson insists on collecting Parliament's tea tax . . . but did we have a vote?"

"No!" the mob replied.

"It's time for us to band together as Sons of Liberty," Sam Adams told them. "It's time for us to become Patriots. And Patriots are men of action! Are you with me?" he demanded.

The men went wild with excitement, raising their fists high in the air, and hoisting Sam Adams on their shoulders.

A large, burly man, who'd been standing near the bar listening, suddenly took his pipe from his mouth. He dumped the ashes onto the bar and smeared them on his face in a single thick line. The crowd knew exactly what he meant.

That was not just any symbol. That stripe was an Indian war stripe. The time had come for the people of Boston to fight back.

Within moments, the mob had taken to the streets. Men disguised as Indians, carrying axes, joined together and headed for the harbor. As they made their way to the water, they barely noticed the small chariot with the broken axle.

Moses gestured for Henri and James to stay back and remain hidden in the shadows.

"Indians, James," Henri whispered in a small, frightened voice. "Moses, Mohawk Indians."

But Moses knew better. He pointed to a tall blond man dressed in warpaint and an Indian headdress. "A Mohawk with yellow hair?" he wondered aloud. No, these weren't Indians. There was something else brewing in the streets of Boston.

"There's a story here," James suggested to Moses. "Let's see where they lead us."

Moses nodded in agreement. Quickly, he and the boys took off on foot after the mob, making sure to stay far enough away not to be discovered.

It didn't take long to figure out where the angry men were headed. Sam Adams led the group to the docks, and helped them silently slip small rowboats into the water. One by one, groups of disguised colonists climbed into the boats, and began rowing into the harbor.

There was no time to waste.

"They're headed for the *Dartmouth*," Moses whispered to James and Henri. "We've got to find Sarah, fast!"

## Chapter Four

The sea was dark. The night was quiet. Everything seemed still and motionless until . . . suddenly, a man's arm appeared over the railing on the deck of the *Dartmouth*. Quickly, Sam Adams hoisted himself onto the ship. A mob of colonists, dressed as Indians, followed close behind.

Suddenly the silence of the night was broken by loud, ferocious Indian war cries. The colonists were worked up and angry, and they weren't afraid to let everyone know it.

The men were so focused on their mission, they didn't notice that another boat had pulled up alongside the *Dartmouth*. This one carried two boys and a man—Henri, James, and Moses. At the first sound of screaming, James knew he had a mission. This was the big scoop he'd been waiting for. The one that would finally earn him the reporter's status he'd craved for so long. "You get Sarah," he told Moses and Henri as he began to scramble out of the boat. "I'm going to get the story."

As Moses and Henri scrambled up to the deck of the *Dartmouth*, Sam Adams was warning his men to be careful. "Just the tea, men!" he reminded them. "Remember, we're not to damage anything else. We're just after the tea."

The action was definitely centered around Sam Adams. And James definitely wanted to be in the center of things. The teenager quickly walked right up to the leader and asked pointedly, "Why are you destroying the tea?"

"We're protesting unfair taxation," Sam Adams explained. "Parliament raised the tea tax over our objections. Maybe next time they'll listen."

"Hurrah!" The disguised colonists cheered as they began flinging crates of tea in the harbor. Some of the men swung their axes and split the cases open. Others rolled kegs of tea leaves over the sides of the boat. As

each keg or crate hit the water, it was greeted by a chorus of cheers. Before long, the water surrounding the *Dartmouth* had turned the color of rich, brown tea.

The British soldiers were nowhere in sight. But Moses knew that the colonists' luck would not last forever. Before long, word would reach the leaders of the soldiers stationed in Massachusetts. They would come and break up the protest. People were going to get arrested; maybe even hurt. There was no time to waste.

"Miss Phillips! Sarah Phillips," Moses shouted as he searched the deck of the *Dartmouth*. "Sarah!"

Henri knew he was supposed to stay close to Moses. But he couldn't help himself. Instead of following Moses, the eight-year-old grabbed a fistful of tea and threw it overboard. It flittered through the air like dark brown confetti. "No taxation without representaion!" Henri screamed in his high-pitched French accent.

James turned to him. "Do you know what that means?"

Henri shook his head sheepishly. "Nope. I heard the others saying it," he admitted.

James wished he could explain to Henri what "no taxation without representation" really meant. But this was no time to sit the boy down and explain how unfair it was that Parliament was taxing everything sold in the Americas, without ever asking the colonists how they felt about the taxes. There was no one in Parliament who represented the colonists, which is what made it all so unfair.

But that was another lesson for another time. Right now, James's eyes were bouncing with excitement. He could barely keep still. "We've stumbled onto the story of a lifetime," the young reporter told Henri. "I'm going below deck to see what's happening. Stay out of trouble." And with that, he ducked down a small hatch and made his way to the belly of the boat.

Henri grabbed another handful of tea leaves and chucked it overboard. "Take that, Parliament!" he shouted. "Whoever you are!"

The below deck of the *Dartmouth* was dark and seemingly empty. The only noises came from above. James could hear shouting, chopping, rolling, and splashing as pounds of tea were thrust into the ocean. The footsteps from the upper deck thundered in his ears. James quickly lit a candle and moved deeper into the ship.

*Wham!* Suddenly, James felt something whack him over the head. He crumbled to the floor in pain.

"Take that!" a girl's voice called out in the darkness.

James lifted his head from the floor. "What hit me?" he murmured as he looked around. For a moment, all he saw were feathers flying around the lower deck. Then his eyes fell on a redheaded girl about his own age. She was dressed in fine traveling clothes, although her jacket was hanging crookedly from her shoulder. In her arms she held a pillow that had been split in two.

James felt his head. For a girl, she packed quite a punch—especially since it appeared she'd hit him with nothing more than a feather pillow!

"You'll never take me alive!" Sarah Phillips assured James.

"Take you where?" James asked, rubbing the rapidly growing lump on his head.

"Wherever Indians take people," Sarah said. She lowered the pillow slightly, not sure if this was a trap.

"I'm not no Indian. None of us are," James assured her.

Sarah looked relieved. She wasn't in any danger. She put her hand disapprovingly on her hip. "You're not *an* Indian," she corrected him. "Who taught you grammar?"

James glared at her. "Who taught you to whack people on the head?" he demanded.

Sarah reached into the torn pillow and yanked out a thick hardback book. Considering the size of that book, it was no wonder James had gone down the way he had. This girl could take care of herself.

Sarah pretended not to notice the way James was staring at her. She stood tall, tried to look dignified, and fixed her jacket.

"My apologies," she told James in her very proper British accent. "I thought you were here to kidnap me."

James scrambled to his feet and pulled his charcoal and paper from his pocket. "Kidnap? I'm a reporter for *The Pennsylvania Gazette,*" he informed her proudly, sounding very official. "What do you have to say about the tax protest?"

"Is that what this is about?" Sarah demanded. She waved her hands in the air, using them to punctuate every point she was making. "Disgraceful! The tea is private property. This is so uncivilized! If you were any kind of Englishman you'd drop that charcoal and put a stop to it."

But James had no intention of stopping now. He was a reporter and he was going to get his story. "So you think it's okay to impose taxes on the colonies, even thought the colonies don't have a vote in Parliament?" he asked her.

Sarah put her hand on her hip and rolled her eyes. She was obviously unimpressed with this young man.

"I think loyal subjects of the king should obey the laws of their country. And you can quote me on that—Mister—what is your name?"

"Hiller. James Hiller," he told her. "And who would I be quoting?

"*Whom* may I be quoting," Sarah corrected him. "If you're going to be writing for a newspaper, you really should treat words with more care."

James glared at her. Just who did this girl think she was, anyway? "Tell me your name, will you?" he demanded. "I have work to do."

"Phillips," Sarah replied proudly in a proper English accent. "Miss Sarah Phillips of London, England."

"S-a-r-a-h P-h-i . . . ," James began, spelling the name as he scribbled it down. He stopped suddenly and stared at her. "Sarah Phillips!" he exclaimed. "You're Sarah Phillips?"

Sarah nodded.

James held the candle close to her face to get a good look. "I can't believe you're Sarah Phillips," he told her.

"I am," Sarah assured him. Her voice sounded annoyed and slightly haughty. "And I'll thank you to stop shouting, Mr. Hiller. I've had a very rude welcome to America, and you're not making things any better."

James nodded happily. He was relieved to have found Sarah so quickly. The girl looked at him curiously. That was not at all the expression she'd been expecting.

"We've been looking for you," James explained.

"Have you?" Sarah asked, trying to keep her voice sounding as casual as possible. "And why is that?"

James's smile broadened. He loved the fact that while he knew who Sarah was, she had no idea who he was. Finally, he let her in on the secret. "Benjamin Franklin sent us."

At first, Sarah didn't quite understand. And then, as James's meaning became clear, the shock registered on her face. She was going to be living in the same house with this rude young man. "Dr. Franklin sent you?" she asked in disbelief.

James grinned. "Now who's yelling?" he asked, with a slight laugh. James really did love having the upper hand.

But there wasn't time for James to enjoy Sarah's predicament. There was big trouble on the horizon.

# ★ ★ ★

# Chapter Five

## ★ ★ ★

"Red Coats!" Sam Adams cried out to his men. "Abandon ship! Abandon ship!"

The colonists raced around the deck and began diving into the icy water below. It was better to freeze than to be caught by British soldiers.

Henri was confused and frightened. All around him, men were screaming and leaping into the water. Without James or Moses beside him, the boy was overwhelmed. He didn't know which way to turn or where to go. Frantically, he began to run to the other side of the deck. As he rounded the corner he ran smack into a tall African-American man who'd been running in the opposite direction.

Moses! Henri had never been so glad to see anyone in his entire life.

"Henri!" Moses greeted the boy. "We have to get out of here." He looked around. "Where's James?" he asked.

"Below deck."

The last thing Moses wanted to do was be onboard the *Dartmouth* when the Red Coats arrived. But he knew that he had to find James before they could leave the ship. He couldn't leave Benjamin Franklin's apprentice behind. He quickly pulled Henri along as he raced off toward the nearest hatch.

It didn't take long for Moses to find James. All he had to do was follow the sound of the teenager's angry voice as it echoed loudly through the deck.

"It is *not* a mistake!" Moses heard the boy shout out.

Moses found James in a small, dark room. He was apparently having quite an argument with an obviously wealthy young lady. This was no time for James to be discussing anything with anyone. There was too much danger above.

"James, come on," Moses urged when he spotted the apprentice. "The Red Coats are on their way."

James grabbed Sarah's hand and tried to pull her out of the room. But she fought him with every inch of strength.

"Unhand me!" Sarah demanded.

Moses instantly recognized the young woman's very proper British accent. Based on her clothing, her red hair, and the tone of her voice, he knew exactly who James's sparring partner must be. Moses walked over and smiled kindly in her direction. "Miss Sarah, I presume. Thank goodness we found you."

It was clear from the expression of her face that Sarah was surprised to hear this man say her name. After all, she'd never seen him before in her life.

"If we're caught by those soldiers, we'll be thrown in jail," James told her.

"Which, in my opinion, is exactly where traitors belong," Sarah replied, sounding every bit like the daughter of a distinguished British soldier.

*Bam!* Suddenly, musket fire erupted on the deck above. The British soldiers had arrived, and they seemed to be shooting without asking questions.

James grabbed Sarah and spun her around. He wrapped his strong arms around hers and trapped her in a bear hug. "Sorry, Sarah," he said as he dragged her up the stairs behind Moses and Henri. "But I can't print my story from jail."

"Let me go!" Sarah demanded, struggling to free herself.

But James wouldn't let go. He dragged her to the ship's gangplank.

"Put me down!" Sarah insisted. "Put me down now!"

"I'd love to," James assured her. "But Dr. Franklin told us to take care of you."

Moses pointed to a narrow dock that was next to the gangway. "This way!" he shouted to James as he and Henri raced down the ramp toward the dock.

But pulling Sarah had slowed James down considerably. No sooner had he gotten halfway down the gangplank than a Red Coat soldier darted toward him!

"James, look out!" Moses shouted.

But it was too late. The soldier grabbed for James and Sarah. His hand swept around Sarah's neck, but he couldn't get a grip on either teenager.

The soldier reached for the teens again, but James was too quick for him. He shoved Sarah down the plank toward the dock. She fell and rolled away from James's grasp. Instantly, Moses raced to Sarah's side and pulled her to her feet. In one swift motion, he handed her over into Henri's care.

The soldier looked down at his hand. He was holding a small gold locket in his fingers. He'd torn it from Sarah's neck during the scuffle. The Red Coat had no use for a necklace. He tossed it into the harbor and shook a fist in the air. "Halt! That's an order!" the Red Coat demanded.

But James didn't stop. Instead, he charged across the dock and slammed into the soldier. The Red Coat was caught by surprise. He fell to the ground with James on top of him. The two began to struggle for control. The soldier glared up at James with determination in his eyes. "I'll get you for this," he swore between gasps of air.

James leaped off of the soldier. The Red Coat sprang into action. He reached up, grabbed a thick rope that was tied to a post, and struggled to pull himself to his feet as he stared angrily at James.

The soldier was so focused on his fifteen-year-old opponent that he never saw the colonist who snuck up behind him, ax in hand. In a split second the colonist chopped the rope in half.

"*Aaaah!*" The soldier lost his balance and fell into the cold water.

James smiled gratefully at his rescuer. "No taxation without representation!" the young reporter exclaimed.

✯ ✯ ✯

James barely dared to breathe as Moses led him, along with Henri and Sarah, along the icy docks. It wasn't until he found himself hiding behind a small customs shack that James allowed himself to realize what a close call he'd just experienced—and what an amazing moment of history he'd been a part of.

"Is everyone all right?" Moses asked. All right wasn't the term for it.

"That was fun!" Henri exclaimed.

"What a story!" James declared. "This is headline news!"

"Shhh, lower your voices," Moses warned the boys. "We're not out of the woods yet."

Suddenly Sarah stood up and moved to the edge of the dock. She opened her mouth wide and began to scream, "Heeeeeeelllllllp!"

Instantly, James leaped to his feet and grabbed Sarah from behind. He clamped his hand tightly against her mouth. "Are you crazy?" he demanded. "Do you want the British to catch us?"

Sarah wheeled around and faced James. "I am British," she told him. "We're all British."

Moses looked her intently in the eye. "Right now, those soldiers think we're criminals," he explained.

Sarah gulped. Suddenly she felt frightened, and very far from home. Her mouth moved, but no sound came out. She nodded grimly.

"Criminals?" James demanded. "What did we do wrong?"

"We were in the wrong place at the wrong time," Moses replied. He pointed to a nearby narrow road. "The chariot's over there. Let's go."

No one said a word as they followed Moses to their carriage. James and Sarah both knew that this was no time for arguments. No matter what they each felt about what had they had just seen, both teens were on the same side for the time being. It was the only way they'd be able to escape.

# Chapter Six

James, Henri, and Sarah crouched down and kept themselves pressed against the side of their carriage as Moses stood in the front, steering the horses down the narrow streets.

"Keep down," Moses whispered. "The Red Coats will recognize you three, but I'll just be another faceless servant." It was a sad fact, but he knew it to be true. Black men didn't mean much to the Red Coats. The British soldiers merely assumed that all African Americans were servants. It didn't matter to them whether they were slaves, or freed men like Moses. It was an unfortunate reality that many of the colonists shared that view as well.

As the carriage wobbled along on its broken axle, Sarah glared at James. "Even if you don't like the laws, you can't just ignore them," she insisted. "That will lead to chaos."

"But what if the law is unjust?" James whispered.

"Parliament would never pass an unjust law."

James shook his head in disbelief. "But they have! I interviewed the men tonight." He pulled his notebook from his jacket pocket. "The colonies must pay taxes to the king, but we have no voice in Parliament," James read. "Does that sound fair to you?" he demanded.

It was all so confusing. Sarah had been in America less than one day and already everything she'd ever believed to be true was being challenged. "I don't know what to think," she admitted. "I only know Ben Franklin would hardly approve of what went on tonight."

James leaned back against the side of chariot. "Then you don't know Ben Franklin," he said.

Before Sarah could respond, Moses whispered, "Quick! Get down! The constable."

Instantly, James, Henri, and Sarah ducked down and pulled some old blankets over their heads.

"Be still," Moses warned them, "or it's jail for us all."

The constable walked out in front of the carriage and

blocked the road. "Halt!" he commanded.

Moses did as he was told. He stopped the chariot, taking care to keep the carriage in semidarkness. He didn't want to take any chances. "Good evening, Constable," Moses greeted him. "Fine night."

"Fine night for troublemakers," the constable harrumphed. "State your business."

"I'm just bringing some freshly quartered hogs to the Wheatley residence. That's all."

The constable looked doubtful. "Hogs, say you? At this time of night? I think I'll have myself a look."

Moses dipped his head slightly and gave the constable an unsure look. "I wouldn't if I were you," he said politely. "These are some big, ugly hogs. Nasty to look at. And boy, do they ever smell!"

The constable sniffed at the air. He made a face and stepped away from the chariot. "You're right, they do stink," he agreed. He pointed to the right. "The Wheatley home is right around the corner. Hurry along now. The Red Coats have Boston under curfew. Nobody's allowed on the streets after dark."

Moses nodded. "Won't happen again. Much obliged, sir." Then, without wasting another second, he shook the reins and led the chariot away.

$$\star \quad \star \quad \star$$

# Chapter Seven

$$\star \quad \star \quad \star$$

The Wheatley house was a stately city home, large and elegant. It was impossible not to be impressed with its stature.

But Moses wasn't interested in architecture at the moment. Instead, he was concerned with the safety of the three children hidden in the back of the chariot. He pulled the carriage to a stop and hopped from his seat. "This is the place," he told James, Henri, and Sarah. "Come on."

The three climbed obediently from the rear of the carriage. They waited in the shadows while Moses knocked on a small door at the side of the house.

"Moses, how do you know the Wheatleys?" James

whispered curiously. "You've never been to Boston."

The African-American man smiled. "I don't know the Wheatleys," he admitted. "But all of my people know Phillis Wheatley."

"How?" Henri asked.

"From her poetry. She's the finest poet in the land." He began to recite the woman's poems with a reverence the boys had never before heard in his voice. "'Muse! Where shall I being the spacious field to tell what curses unbelief doth yield.'" Moses stopped his recitation and smiled at the children. "A woman who can write like that would never turn away someone who needs help."

Sarah looked curiously at the side of the house. "Why are we at the servants' door?" she wondered aloud.

Before Moses could reply, the door opened and a beautiful, twenty-year-old African-American woman appeared. "Yes?" she asked sleepily.

"Miss Wheatley?" Moses asked hopefully.

"Yes?"

"We're in trouble, Miss Wheatley," Moses explained.

Just then, Henri snuck up beside Moses. "And we're hungry!" he added, unable to hide his feelings a moment longer.

Phillis Wheatley didn't respond right away. Instead,

she lifted her lantern and peered around for anyone who might be listening. "Did Mr. Adams send you?" she asked in a whisper so quiet, she could barely be heard.

"Um, yes?" James lied.

Phillis nodded. "There's a stable around back," she told the group. "The door squeaks, so be careful. We can't wake the master."

Sarah's big blue eyes opened wide. "You're a slave?" she asked, her British-sounding voice scaling up with surprise.

Phillis didn't answer. Instead, she turned to Moses. "Go. I'll bring some food."

Henri was glad they would be eating soon. His stomach grumbled with anticipation.

But Sarah had suddenly lost her appetite. Even some time later, long after Phillis had brought the group a hearty meal of chicken and homemade bread, and provided their horse, Caesar, with a stack of hay to chomp on, the girl couldn't seem to swallow a bite. An amazing woman like Phillis Wheatley, a slave. It seemed impossible to believe.

And yet it was true.

"We'll never make it back to Philadelphia on this axle," Moses told the others, between bites of bread.

"It has to be replaced."

"Good," James replied. "I'd like to stick around Boston. This is where the action is."

Henri wasn't going to argue with that. "Me too!" he exclaimed as he sucked the last bit of meat from a drumstick. "If Miss Wheatley can write half as good as she cooks, she must be another Shakespeare!" He reached for a drumstick on James's plate. But James was quicker. He slapped Henri's hand away.

Sarah set her plate down. "How can a woman like Phillis Wheatley be somebody's property?" she asked "It's outrageous!"

Moses sat back quietly on his heels. He listened but did not say a word.

"Those men tonight, throwing tea into the water— all that talk of freedom. What about freedom for Miss Wheatley?" Sarah insisted.

"Not everyone in the colonies believes in slavery, Sarah," James assured her.

Sarah frowned. "Talk is easy."

"And freedom is priceless," Moses interrupted suddenly.

James, Henri, and Sarah stared at him.

"I know; I was born free, in West Africa. But when I was not much bigger than little Henri here, my brother and I were captured and chained to the decks of a ship." His eyes misted over as he remembered. "An awful ship—for the long voyage to Virginia and slavery."

"That's terrible, Moses," Sarah said sympathetically. "How did you escape?"

Moses held his hands up in front of his face. "I escaped by using my head and my hands. I learned smithing, a valuable skill. My master loaned me out for odd jobs here and there, and sometimes I was given silver coins for my work. When I earned enough coins, I bought my freedom back and traveled to Philadelphia." He smiled, recalling the cleverness of his plan. "There I learned to read and write, and was offered a job by Dr. Franklin, a man who hates slavery as much as I do."

Sarah seemed confused. "Moses, how can you support those rebels?" she asked him. "In England, slavery is dying. Here it's thriving. Think of poor Phillis."

It was a legitimate question. The colonists were crying for their freedom, even as their slaves tended their farms and cleaned their homes for them.

Moses stood up and focused on the broken chariot axle as he considered his words. "I believe America's struggle is like my own," he replied finally. "The colonists consider themselves enslaved to a master they did not choose. And that's a fight. If it comes to fighting, I will not duck."

For a moment, no one said a word. The only sound in the barn was Moses's hammer as it banged against the chariot's broken axle.

Finally, Henri was the one to speak. "I'll fight you for that drumstick," he told James. Quickly, the little French boy snatched the chicken leg from James's plate. James swung at him, but he was too late. Henri bit into the juicy chicken meat and grinned triumphantly. Even Moses couldn't help but laugh at Henri's quick thinking.

"It's very late," Moses told the children. "We should get some sleep." He reached over and blew out the lantern beside him. Suddenly the barn went dark. "Good night, all."

Within an instant, Moses, James, and Henri were asleep, nestled quietly against the soft hay on the barn floor. But Sarah was troubled. She tossed and turned as thoughts ran through her mind. *Father, I know you came here to buy land and make a better life for us, she thought. But wherever you are, I pray you are safe. I pray you will return from the west so we can be a family again.*

Sarah reached up to feel the locket she always wore around her neck. For the first time, she realized it had disappeared. "My locket!" she exclaimed. "It's gone!"

Sarah felt utterly and completely alone.

4, January, 1774

Dearest Mother,

So much has happened since I have arrived, I barely know where to start. I'm so confused. These Americans speak of liberty and freedom for all, but deny it to those with skin different from their own. I only hope that everything will be all right once Dr. Franklin arrives. I trust that all is well with him.

We live in a barn, fugitives from His Majesty's soldiers, sheltered by a remarkable woman, a poet and slave named Phillis Wheatley. James, Henri, and Moses support these radicals, but I for one can't wait to leave Boston.

When is Ben Franklin coming? Soon, I hope. Very soon!

Your loyal, loving daughter,
Sarah

# Chapter Eight

Sarah sat alongside the Wheatleys' barn as she quickly dashed off yet another letter to her mother. Writing home filled her with emotions. In some ways, it made her feel closer to her mum. In other ways, it made the distance between them seem endless.

She'd been in America only a short while, and already she'd experienced more fear, confusion, and excitement than she had in her entire life.

Sarah looked down at her traveling clothes. Her gold-colored traveling suit was torn at the hem and filthy with dirt from sleeping on the barn floor. She reached up and pulled a stalk of hay from her knotted red hair. Then she put her hand to her neck and felt where her locket used to be. What would her mother say if she could see her now?

☆ ☆ ☆

But Lady Phillips had larger matters on her mind than her daughter's unruly appearance. Her dear friend Benjamin Franklin was in big trouble. At that very moment, Lady Phillips was seated in the balcony gallery of a courtroom known as the cockpit. She and other members of British nobility were witnesses as Dr. Benjamin Franklin was accused of treason!

Lady Phillips listened carefully as Solicitor General Alexander Wedderburn, dressed in his elegant crimson robes and formal powdered wig, faced Benjamin Franklin on the floor of the courthouse and attacked his character.

"Benjamin Franklin, Benjamin Franklin. The great Dr. Franklin," Solicitor General Wedderburn bellowed, his voice dripping with sarcasm. "Friend of humanity! Inventor of the lightning rod! Father of electricity! Author of *Poor Richard's Almanack*! Deputy postmaster general for North America!"

Solicitor General Wedderburn looked up at the

assembly of dukes and lords seated in the gallery. It was obvious he was playing to the crowd. Benjamin Franklin stared straight ahead, unflinching.

Wedderburn pointed his finger dramatically at Ben. "Yes, he is all these things," he declared. "But he is something more. . . . He is a traitor! I charge Dr. Franklin with instigating the Boston Tea Riot! And for his crime, he must pay the price!"

Lady Phillips gasped. She knew the price for treason. If he was convicted as a traitor, Benjamin Franklin could go to jail or worse!

"On the evening of sixteen December, the year of our Lord seventeen seventy-three, cowardly bandits, disguised as Indians, attacked the *Dartmouth*, a ship flying the colors of His Majesty, King George III," Solicitor General Wedderburn stopped and thrust his finger into Ben's face. Ben stood there, unflinching.

"And who is responsible for inflaming the subjects of Boston to this violence?" Mr. Wedderburn shouted. "None other than the man before us—the esteemed Deputy Postmaster Benjamin Franklin!"

The lords and ladies who were assembled in the gallery began to boo and hiss. Only Lady Phillips sat quietly, with a worried wrinkle in her brow. Ben looked up at her and gave her an encouraging smile.

Mr. Wedderburn stalked across the room. "His crimes are enormous! The East India Company lost hundreds of crates of tea, worth many thousands of pounds. This lawlessness was encouraged by Dr. Franklin in his speeches and writings. His inflammatory paper, *The Pennsylvania Gazette*, continues to encourage sedition, rebellion, violence, *treason!*"

The word *treason* rang through the gallery. But Ben showed absolutely no emotion as his accuser continued to rant and rave. "You have no honor, sir," Mr. Wedderburn shouted. "You are a scoundrel, sir! Have you nothing to say for yourself?"

Ben Franklin facing Solicitor General Wedderburn

Ben looked straight into Mr. Wedderburn's eyes. "The heart of a fool is in his mouth, but the mouth of a wise man is in his heart."

The lords and ladies of the gallery began to laugh. With a single sentence, Ben had definitely one-upped Mr. Wedderburn.

And Mr. Wedderburn was not pleased. His eyes glared, and his voice became even more sharp and sarcastic. "Ahhh, the famous Franklin wit," he retorted. "Perhaps I need to remind you that a rope is the proper reward for treason?"

For the first time, Ben looked worried. Lady Phillips seemed concerned as well. Without even thinking about it, her hands flew to her throat.

Things were not looking good for Benjamin Franklin.

# Chapter Nine

Of course, Sarah knew nothing about Dr. Franklin's public trial. News from England took more than two months to arrive by ship. At the moment all the girl knew was that she was living in a barn, hiding from soldiers who served the same king her father did. And although they had only been staying in the Wheatleys' barn for a few short weeks, it seemed like years since she'd slept in a proper bed or had clean water to wash with. And it was so cold. January in Boston was a time filled with snow and grayness.

Sarah sighed. What a way to begin 1774.

Unlike Sarah, James was thrilled with what the new year had offered so far. Being in Boston offered him a close-up view of the revolution that was brewing among the colonists. Each day seemed to bring new acts of rebellion, followed by new efforts by the Red Coats to suppress them. This was truly the story of a lifetime, and the young reporter was taking every opportunity to record what was happening. Each day, he and Henri went to the harbor and tried to find out more about what was going on.

"How many do you see, Henri?" he asked as the two boys stood at the harbor, trying to keep track of the British ships that seemed to be arriving daily. They tried to count the British ships.

Henri was perched on James's shoulders, which gave the little guy a clear view of the harbor. "*Un, deux, trois, quatre, cinq,*" Henri counted in his native French.

"English, Henri," James scolded him. "Not French."

"I am counting the English," Henri insisted.

"How many are there now?" James asked. He was becoming frustrated at not being able to see the action for himself.

Henri looked out onto the long dock. It seemed as

though hundreds of Red Coats were marching toward them. "Too many!" Henri exclaimed. "There mustn't be a soldier left in England!"

Henri watched in amazement as two British soldiers nailed a sign to the rail of the dock. The sign read:

> BOSTON HARBOR CLOSED BY ORDER OF PARLIAMENT!

Quickly, Henri leaped down from James's shoulder. "What should we do?" he asked the older boy nervously.

But James wasn't nervous at all. He was excited. "What should we do?" he asked. "The British are occupying Boston! I've got to get this to the *Gazette* right away! Come on, Henri!"

And with that, the two boys ran off in the direction of the Wheatleys' home. They had to tell Moses what was happening.

☆ ☆ ☆

"Hundreds of new soldiers arrived by ship this morning," James informed Moses and Sarah when the boys arrived back at the barn.

"The whole city is filled with Red Coats," Henri agreed.

"Boston Harbor is closed," James added, unable to

hide the shock and anger in his voice.

At first, Sarah sat quietly to the side. But James's last outburst was more than she could bear. "Would you please mind your tongue?" she insisted. She rolled her eyes toward the barn door, trying to remind James that there were soldiers nearby.

James, Sarah, Henri, and Moses weren't the only people taking advantage of the Wheatleys' hospitality. There were plenty of British soldiers there as well. Luckily, none of them had recognized the children as the ones who had been on the docks in the hours following the Boston Tea Party.

But James didn't get the hint. "Where's my quill?" he asked. "I have a story to write! This is headline news!"

Moses glanced toward the doorway. Henri was standing there, waving to someone, probably some Red Coat soldiers. Many of them had invited themselves to stay in the Wheatleys' home. Not that the Wheatleys would've had the option to say no even if they'd wanted to. That was the law. Colonists had to open their homes to Red Coats. Moses knew that Sarah was right. James had better watch his mouth. The last thing they needed was to upset the soldiers who had taken shelter inside the Wheatleys' home. "Ahem,

James," Moses said, trying to get the boy's attention.

But if James had heard Moses, he chose to ignore him. "Those filthy Red Coats are everywhere," he continued.

Sarah gave James a warning smile. "That's right, James," she began, trying desperately to stop him from saying anything else. "After that long sea voyage, these lovely *red coats* could use a good cleaning." She turned to a coatless soldier who had just entered the barn. "This may need some soap and water," she said, holding his jacket in her hands.

Within a few seconds, five more Red Coats appeared in the barn. They laid their gear out on the bar. They were clearly taking over the place.

The sight of those additional soldiers made even James aware that he would have to be more careful about what he did and said. "Let me help you, Sarah," he said, grabbing a small handbroom and sweeping dust from one of the soldier's coats. "Fine morning, isn't it?" he remarked to the soldier.

But the Red Coat had already heard James's outburst. "'Tis you who could use the soap and water . . . in that smart mouth of yours!" he told James.

James nodded. "You're absolutely right," he agreed, trying to avoid a confrontation. "You'll have to forgive my manners. I'm an orphan. I was raised on the streets and sometimes forget my place." It killed James to have to speak that way, but getting along with the soldiers was clearly a matter of survival.

"Where's that grub we was promised?" the soldier demanded, apparently unmoved by James's confession.

"I'll check on it right away, sir," Sarah promised. She grabbed James and Henri by the collars of their shirts. "Why don't you come give me a hand in the kitchen?" she suggested to the boys.

James scowled. "The kitchen? That's women's work."

Sarah gave James a swift kick to the shin. That got his attention. "The kitchen! Of course!" he corrected himself. "It would be an honor to help, me lady." He bowed to the soldiers as he left the barn and followed Sarah toward the kitchen.

As Moses and the three children walked to the house, James looked curiously at Sarah. "You're on their side. Why didn't you turn us in?" he whispered.

"I would if I thought I wouldn't end up in jail with you," Sarah replied simply.

Moses and the children found Phillis in the kitchen stirring a huge pot in the fireplace. James had never seen such a large kitchen. The fireplace took up almost an entire wall. The pantry was stocked with cheeses hanging from the ceiling, and the shelves were well stocked with food.

James pulled a cheese from the ceiling and walked over to Sarah. "What are the Red Coats doing in the barn?" he asked her.

"It's called 'quartering,'" Phillis explained. "A soldier just knocks on your door, anytime, day or night, and moves into your house. We have five more upstairs. Master Wheatley is very upset."

"I can't believe King George would allow that," Sarah argued.

James and Sarah might have been concerned about the presence of so many soldiers, but Henri could only focus on the pie Sarah had just placed in a basket for the soldiers. When the older children weren't looking, the little French boy swiped the pie and began digging in to the sweet fruity filling with a fork.

"It's Parliament's doing," Phillis continued. "They call it the Intolerable Acts, and quartering is the least of it."

"This is an outrage!" James declared.

"That's right," Phillis agreed. "We have to cook for them, wash their clothes, and they don't have to pay a single shilling."

Sarah looked curiously at Phillis. It seemed odd to her that the slave woman would be so supportive of the rebels. "You're already doing that for *Master* Wheatley," she reminded her.

James looked at Phillis, wondering how she would react to Sarah's statement. But Phillis didn't seem to be outraged by Sarah's views. She simply kept cooking, calmly.

"I'm outraged," Henri piped in suddenly. The others looked at him, surprised. "This pie is too small!" he declared, showing them a near-empty pie tin.

"They say it's because of the tea party," Phillis told James. "I heard Lieutenant Brampton tell Master Wheatley, 'If Boston's going to cause trouble, Boston's going to pay the piper.'"

"That only makes sense," Sarah agreed.

James couldn't believe his ears. He leaned his face toward Sarah's. "Whose side are you on?" he demanded.

Sarah leaned her face toward James's. "I didn't know there were sides. We're all the king's subjects," she reminded him.

But James wasn't having any of that. "Maybe you're a subject," he insisted, "but I'm a citizen. I have rights!"

Sarah pointed toward Phillis. "Doesn't Phillis have rights?" she demanded.

Henri looked over at the two feuding teenagers. He smiled at Sarah, as if to say, "That was a good one." But he didn't utter a sound. His mouth was too full of pie to speak.

"You know what your problem is, Sarah?" James demanded.

"Besides you," Sarah spat back.

"You think too much for a girl," James told her.

Sarah was not taking talk like that lying down. "And you talk too much for a gentleman."

Seeing that he wasn't going to win any arguments with Sarah today, James switched his focus. He turned to Phillis. "I need a printing press," he told her. "I've got to get word out."

Sarah interrupted before Phillis could even respond. "James, until Moses can fix the chariot, we're stuck here," she reminded him. "The city is swarming with soldiers who would like nothing better than to arrest us for your *tea party*. So unless you plan on printing us tickets to Philadelphia, I suggest you keep your nose clean."

"I'll clean my nose after I get the word out," James informed her.

Phillis looked worriedly toward the door, making sure there were no Red Coats listening. Once she was sure they were alone in the kitchen, she reached into her pocket and pulled out a key. "Take this, James," she whispered. "Tom Maloney published my poems. I can use his press anytime. His shop is on Bay Street. Hurry!"

James ignored Sarah's stern frown as he took the key from Phillis's work-worn hands. "Bay Street. Got it!" he repeated.

Phillis shot Moses a worried glance. James didn't seem to be grasping the danger involved in what he planned to do.

"James, be careful," Moses warned.

"I'm not afraid," James replied, puffing his chest up like a proud peacock. He held up his quill. "The pen is mightier than the sword."

"True, but the Red Coats have muskets," Phillis reminded him.

James stopped smiling. He nodded gravely. "I'll be careful, I promise," he assured her.

"You're forgetting one small detail," Sarah reminded the others. "There's a barn full of soldiers waiting for us to return with food."

Phillis lifted the heavy tureen from the fireplace and gave the food a final stir. Then she pulled a giant roast turkey from the oven. "This ought to do the trick,"

Phillis said as she placed the golden bird on a platter.

"After this feast, they'll be out like a candle," Henri agreed.

The sooner the soldiers fell asleep, the sooner James could sneak out to the printer's. "Let's go," he urged the others.

Phillis quickly opened the back door and walked toward the barn with the turkey. Moses, Sarah, James, and Henri grabbed the rest of the food and followed close behind.

# Chapter Ten

Phillis Wheatley was a very smart woman. Sure enough, her big turkey dinner was all it took to get the Red Coats tired enough for an afternoon nap. As soon as they were peacefully snoring away, James headed for Maloney's Print Shop. Sarah and Henri tagged along, to act as lookouts as James did his work.

Unlike Philadelphia, Boston was a city of steep hills, and Bay Street was no exception. Usually it was a busy street, lined with shops of all sorts. But today, all of the stores were closed.

Finally, the trio reached Maloney's Print Shop. The

store was located at the bottom of the hill, on the corner. It may have been a good location for a store owner, but it was not convenient for James's mission. There were too many directions the Red Coats could surprise them from.

Still, James knew he had to print his story. He knocked on the door. "Mr. Maloney?" he called. "Tom Maloney? Open up! We're friends of Phillis Wheatley."

But there was no answer.

Henri cupped his hands and peered in through the shop window. "No one is in there," he told the others.

James knew why all the shops were closed. "Today's the Sabbath," he said.

"The Lord's Day," Henri added.

A grin started to form on James's face. "Well, the Lord helps those who help themselves," he said mischievously. He took the key out of his pocket and put it in the lock.

That caught Sarah's attention. "What are you doing?" Sarah demanded.

"Relax," James replied. "Phillis gave us the key." He turned the key and opened the door. "Ladies first," he added as he stepped aside to let Sarah enter.

"At last, a sign of manners," she said as she walked into the shop.

James and Henri followed quickly behind her, drawing the drapes over the windows. They made their way to the presses.

"Red Coats!" James reminded them. "We have to work fast!"

The others knew James was right. The soldiers in the barn couldn't sleep forever. They would soon discover that the kids were missing.

★ ★ ★

As the soldiers slept, Moses continued to work on the axle of the chariot wheel. He wanted to return to Philadelphia before things got much worse in Boston. When he finally felt that the wheel had been straightened as well as it could be, he placed it back onto the chariot. But before he could turn a single screw or fasten a bolt, the wheel slipped off the axle and rolled across the barn . . . right over the stomach of one of the sleeping soldiers.

No turkey dinner in the world could have helped the soldier sleep through that! He woke with a start. "What? Who goes there?" he demanded, looking around. Beside him were the other sleeping soldiers. Only Moses was awake.

"Where'd them kids go off to?" the Red Coat demanded.

Moses struggled to remain calm. "I've been busy

doing my chores," he said in a slow, measured voice. "I'm sure they're around here somewhere."

The soldier's eyes narrowed suspiciously. He grabbed his musket and poked the other sleeping soldiers in the side. "Nigel, Basil, Chauncy," he ordered. "On your feet."

The soldiers awakened slowly. They looked at their fellow Red Coat through groggy eyes.

"Those little troublemakers have run off. The city is under martial law," the soldier reminded them. "They're breaking curfew. We'd better fetch Lieutenant Brampton."

At the very mention of their commanding officer, the soldiers sprang to attention. They grabbed their muskets and rushed from the barn, leaving Moses to himself.

I've got to warn James, Moses thought as he, too, ran off.

Lieutenant Brampton wasn't surprised to hear about the missing children. He knew exactly who the troublemakers must be. "I'll bet they're the same kids who got away during the Tea Riot. But they won't get away a second time," he assured his men.

As the large group of soldiers rode off on horseback in search of the three children, James and Henri were wasting no time getting their work done. The boys were running the printing press at top speed. Already there was a huge stack of posters on the floor in front of them. The message on the poster was quite clear. It read:

**WARNING! PARLIAMENT PASSES INTOLERABLE ACTS**

Underneath that headline James had listed all of the Intolerable Acts that forced the colonists to open their homes to the soldiers.

"Keep going, Henri," James urged.

"Aye-aye, sir," Henri agreed, playfully saluting James. He kept working.

James walked over toward the window, where Sarah was busy peering through the drapes. He looked over her head at the dark street. "The sun's set," he said. "Good. It's time to spread the word."

Sarah didn't answer. She just kept looking out the window, her face set in a worried frown.

"What's wrong, Sarah?" James asked.

She turned and looked him in the eye. "James, are you really an orphan?" she asked softly. "I heard you tell the soldiers before."

James let the curtain drop from his hands. "It's true," he said slowly. "Mother and Father didn't have one of Dr. Franklin's newfangled lightning rods. Our house was struck and burst into flames. It burned to the ground. I was lucky. A neighbor pulled me out in the nick of time." He stopped for a minute. It had been many years ago, but the thought of it still hurt. "Dr. Franklin's lightning rod has saved thousands of lives," he added finally. "When I was old enough I sought him out. He offered to take me in as his apprentice, and I've been working at the *Gazette* ever since."

Sarah reached up to her neck, where her locket had once been. She blushed. "I'm sorry for complaining about a silly locket, when you've lost so much more," she told him sincerely.

"That locket meant a lot, huh?" James said.

Sarah nodded slowly. "My father gave it to me before he sailed for America. When it was around my neck it was like having him near me always."

"You're worried about him."

Sarah peered out the window again. "He went up the Ohio River," she explained as she looked into the darkness. "When he returns, my mother, sister, and brother will join us here. But we haven't heard a word from father in nearly a year."

James held out his hand to her. A shimmering gold band sat on his finger. "See this?" he said gently.

"It's beautiful."

"It's my mother's ring," James told Sarah. "So you see, I know just how you feel about the locket."

Sarah smiled. It was the first time she'd felt any connection to James or to anyone else in America. It was nice to know there was someone who understood.

Suddenly, a small French voice piped up from across the room. "James, I'm done."

The two teens turned to see Henri looking pitifully tiny beside a huge pile of freshly printed posters. Instantly, James snapped back into command-mode. "Grab a stack, Henri," he ordered. "It's time to go."

"Must you do this?" Sarah pleaded. "You'll only make things worse."

But James had already made up his mind. "I have to," he insisted.

"Why?"

James grabbed a stack of posters. "Because, as Dr. Franklin's friend Edmund Burke said, 'An Englishman is the unfittest person on earth to argue another Englishman into slavery.' "

As James and Henri raced out of the print shop, posters in hand, Sarah put her fingers to her empty neck. "Father, where are you? What have I walked into? Oh, where are you, Dr. Franklin?" she cried out. "If only you were here to stop this madness."

# Chapter Eleven

Dr. Franklin was facing his own kind of madness back in London. And his life lay in the balance. At the moment, Wedderburn was giving his closing statement to those assembled in the courthouse. "In summary, my lords, Benjamin Franklin, the deputy postmaster of His Majesty's colonies, is a traitor," he declared.

The crowd booed Dr. Franklin. There was no doubt where their loyalties lay.

Mr. Wedderburn picked up a packet of papers and waved them dramatically. "The proof is in his own words, his own writings. And for this treachery, I ask that as a minimum he be stripped of his position as postmaster and that he bear the stigma and shame of a scoundrel disloyal to king and country."

As Mr. Wedderburn paused to take a breath, the crowd took up his cause. "Traitor . . . traitor . . . traitor," they chanted. Only Lady Phillips sat quietly in the balcony, blotting her tears with her handkerchief.

Slowly, Benjamin Franklin stood. He bowed with respect to the lords in the gallery and to his rival, Mr. Wedderburn. He began to speak in a calm, clear voice. "From the bottom of my heart, I thank Mr. Wedderburn for everything he has said against me."

A statement like that couldn't help but catch everyone's attention—especially Alexander Wedderburn's. "What kind of trick is this?" the solicitor general demanded.

Ben Franklin looked up at the gallery, and then addressed Mr. Wedderburn directly. "My gratitude is sincere," he assured him. "You have answered a question that has troubled me since boyhood. But you have finally put my mind at ease."

Lady Phillips, along with the other nobles in the gallery, seemed shocked at Dr. Franklin's reply to the charges. Ladies ducked behind their fans and flapped wildly, as if trying not faint. Their husbands looked at one another, frowning and murmuring amongst themselves. Ben was well aware of their reaction, but he didn't acknowledge it.

"The question is fundamental," he continued. "And when my fellow colonists arrive at the same answer as I do, a great empire may fall."

At that, Solicitor General Wedderburn spun around to face the lords in the gallery. "More treason!" he spat out.

Ben turned to look at Mr. Wedderburn. He spoke slowly and clearly, as though he were explaining something to a very small boy. "Mr. Wedderburn says I'm a traitor. But this is not true! The question he has answered for me is thus—am I a British subject, or am I the citizen of a new nation? A country distinct and different from England." He paused for a moment, and then addressed the lords and ladies in the balcony. "Today I declare my answer. I am not British. I am an American!"

The crowd let out a gasp of surprise. But Ben wasn't finished yet.

"And a man can only betray his own country," he continued. "My country is no longer England. My country is America!"

★ ★ ★

Back in Ben Franklin's country, things were getting dangerous for Henri and James. The boys didn't know it yet, but the British soldiers had already discovered them. And Lieutenant Brampton was determined to see that this time, they did not escape.

"Hey you! Halt! That's an order!" the lieutenant barked as he spotted Henri nailing one of James's posters to the thick trunk of a tree.

Henri turned and looked over his shoulder. His eyes opened wide with fear.

"Run!" James ordered. Henri did as he was told. Together, the boys raced off, disappearing into the shadows.

"What do we do now?" the little French boy asked as the two hid behind some wooden barrels.

"We pray that Moses has that axle fixed," James told him. He sighed. "Henri, I think we may have overstayed our welcome in Boston."

"How do we get past those Red Coats?" Henri asked nervously.

James thought about that for a moment. "Follow me," he said as he wrapped his arms around one of the huge barrels and began to rock back and forth. The barrel tipped over and began to roll down the steep hill, carrying James with it.

Henri got the message. He, too, began to rock back and forth, until the heavy barrel he was holding fell over as well. It followed right behind the first barrel, picking up speed as it rolled downhill.

At first, the soldiers, who were standing at the bottom of the hill talking to Lieutenant Brampton, didn't notice the two heavy barrels coming right for them. They were too busy searching for James and Henri. And by the time the barrels reached them, it was too late to escape their fate.

"Look out!" Lieutenant Brampton ordered.

The soldiers scattered as the barrels thundered toward them. They ran in every direction, trying to avoid being bowled over. They were so scared, they didn't even hear the boys screaming as they rolled down the hill with their barrels.

*"Whoooaaaaaaa!"*

Lieutenant Brampton regained his footing quickly and jumped on his horse as the barrels rolled off. "Must have fallen off a cart," he told the soldiers. "Come on, men, we have to catch whoever's hanging these posters."

But the boys who had been hanging the posters were long gone, rolling their way down Bay Street toward the print shop. *"Whoaaaa!"* they shouted again as the barrels slammed into the stone wall of the shop and came to an abrupt halt.

"Are you all right, Henri?" James asked, trying to focus his eyes as the world spun around him.

Henri looked up. There seemed to be at least two of everything and everyone. "Which one of you said that?" he asked weakly.

The print shop door swung open, and Sarah came running into the street. "James! Henri! Are you all right?"

The boys tried to stand up, but they were so woozy that their knees buckled beneath them.

Before Henri or James could regain their footing, Moses drove up to the print shop in the chariot. Phillis Wheatley sat by his side.

"Quick, we have to get out of here!" Moses called to the children.

Phillis shook her head and looked up the hill. "Too late," she said.

Lieutenant Brampton and his soldiers were already on their way.

Sarah thought fast. She opened the print shop door. "Everybody inside!" she shouted.

James and Henri wobbled their way into the print shop. Moses and Phillis leaped from the carriage and followed behind. Sarah locked the door. Moses grabbed two chairs and helped Henri and James sit down. He slapped James proudly on the back.

The apprentice had done a good job. He'd alerted the public to the Intolerable Acts, and had managed to take care of Henri at the same time. But now it was time to leave Boston behind. "The chariot is good as new," Moses told the others. "We must leave town. Right now, while it's still dark."

"Amen to that," James agreed.

"After this, I'm never going to roll again—not even in my sleep!" Henri moaned.

*Crash!*

Suddenly the print shop door burst open! The Red Coats rushed inside!

James, Sarah, Henri, Moses, and Phillis froze in their places. They'd been caught. And this time there didn't seem to be any way out!

# Chapter Twelve

Lieutenant Brampton entered the print shop, a triumphant grin on his face. He wandered around the room as though he were a lion stalking his prey. "So, my men and I were riding past this print shop when I heard voices coming from the inside," he said in a strong, proud voice. "So I asked myself, 'What's someone doing in a print shop at this hour, on a Sunday?'" He stopped for a moment, as though he were genuinely expecting an answer.

But James, Sarah, Henri, Moses, and Phillis sat silent, staring into space.

Lieutenant Brampton stood facing James. "You know what I told myself?" he asked him. "I said, 'printing these!'" the lieutenant exclaimed as he pulled one of James's posters from his pocket.

James gulped. This was not good. Putting up posters could be considered treason.

"You have this all wrong, sir," Phillis assured the lieutenant. "These gentlemen are interested in my poetry. They wanted to see where it was published."

Lieutenant Brampton stared at Phillis with disgust and disbelief. "Poetry, you?" he said to the woman, whom he knew to be a slave. "What do you take me for?"

"Show them, Phillis. Go ahead," Moses said.

One of the soldiers choked back a laugh. "Yes. Let's hear this poetry of yours."

Phillis stood proud as she began to recite her own words. " 'Descend to earth, there place thy throne; to succor man's afflicted son. Each human heart inspire: To act in bounties unconfin'd. Enlarge the close contracted mind, and fill it with thy fire.' "

It was hard to argue with Phillis's talent. "Right, so you're a poet," Lieutenant Brampton admitted. "But I still believe these runts have something to do with spreading rebellion, and I aim to find the evidence." He turned to his soldiers and barked out an order. "Tear the place apart if you have to!" He gave James and Henri an evil stare. "If I find so much as one poster, it's jail for the lot of you!"

As the soldiers began to ransack the print shop, the determined lieutenant rested his eyes on Sarah. "You!" he demanded.

". . . Me?" Sarah said in a small voice.

"What's your name?"

"Sarah Phillips, sir."

Lieutenant Brampton paused for a moment. "Phillips, do you say?" he asked. "I served under a Major Phillips during the Seven Years' War."

"Major Phillips is my father, sir."

Lieutenant Brampton leaned back and nodded slowly. "Then you're an Englishwoman, Sarah. It's your duty to tell me who made these posters." He looked her straight in the eye. "The truth, now. Your father would expect you to tell the truth to an officer in the service of his king."

James, Moses, and Phillis all turned and stared at Sarah. Would she turn them in?

Sarah didn't know what to do. She was a loyal servant of the king. But she'd also made a bond with these people. She looked at little Henri, who was staring up with fear in his eyes, at a tall soldier.

"I . . . I . . . I," Sarah stammered nervously.

"Spill it, girl," Lieutenant Brampton insisted.

Sarah lowered her eyes. She was so frightened. She'd

never been in any situation like this before. *Prison?* What would her father say?

That's when she saw it. A poster! Hidden between the leg of the stove and the baseboard of the floor. If she'd spotted it, the soldiers were soon to see it as well.

"Well?" Lieutenant Brampton said, his impatience growing. "I'm waiting, young lady."

Sarah looked up and forced a smile to her nervous lips. "Where are my manners?" she said, sounding every bit a member of the British upper class. "You must be half frozen riding in this cold weather!" She walked closer to the stove. "I'll fix a pot of tea on the stove," she said.

James took a step toward her, but stopped as Lieutenant Brampton glared in his direction. For that one moment the lieutenant took his eyes off of Sarah. And that was all the time she needed.

As she walked near the stove, Sarah bent down and gingerly picked up the poster wedged between the stove and baseboard. Then she quickly tucked it into the

*Franklin Stove*

stove. The flames licked up the evidence in an instant. "There, the fire is stoked," she told the lieutenant. "We'll have hot tea in half a tick. Now what was that you asked me? Something about posters?"

Lieutenant Brampton narrowed his eyes. He was sure Sarah was up to something. The question was, what was it?

Before the lieutenant could ask any more questions, one of his soldiers approached. "Nothing, Lieutenant. The place is clean," he said. "No sign of them signs."

Lieutenant Brampton was furious. "I don't have time for this," he exploded. "Come on, men. The rabble-rousers are getting away while we're dilly-dallying with children and poets and . . . tea!" With that, he stormed out of the print shop. The Red Coats followed close behind.

For a moment, no one spoke. Phillis waited until she was sure the Red Coats were gone before she exclaimed, "Quick! To the chariot! Before they come back!"

Moses looked at her gratefully. "How can we ever thank you?" he asked.

"Keep fighting for freedom, that's how. Now be off!"

She didn't have to ask twice. Moses and the children ran outside and scrambled for the chariot. With a single snap of his leather strap, the horses raced off.

The children hid in the back as Moses nearly flew through the streets of Boston. The motion of the carriage put Henri to sleep immediately. But the two teenagers were too worked up to rest.

"Thank you," James whispered to Sarah.

"For what?"

"You know," James told her.

"I don't know what you're talking about," Sarah said innocently.

"Sure you do. You saved our hides."

Sarah looked at him, expressionless. "James, I'm very tired, and I'm cold."

Immediately, James slipped out of his brown woolen coat. He reached across the carriage and draped it like a blanket over Sarah and Henri. Henri snuggled up inside the blanket. Sarah smiled. "I'm going to make a gentleman of you yet," she told James.

He laughed. "And I am going to make an American out of you."

☆ ☆ ☆

The journey to Philadelphia was long and tedious. By the time they finally reached Dr. Franklin's house, Sarah had gotten to know Moses, James, and Henri well. She respected them, even if she couldn't bring herself to agree with them.

Still, Sarah found it difficult living in a home of

men. They made so much noise sometimes, she could barely think, never mind write a letter home. One afternoon while she was sending off a note to her mother, James was especially loud, banging at something in the print shop with a hammer.

"James! Cut out that racket!" she demanded. "Would you please stop that noise?"

But James refused to stop banging. Sarah threw down her quill and stormed into the print shop. "I'm trying to concentrate!" she shouted over the banging.

Moses looked over at the workbench where James was hammering. "Go ahead, James," he shouted. "It's finished."

James looked up from his project. "Sarah," he said slowly.

"What is it?"

Moses smiled. "The boys have a little something for you."

"For me?" she said.

"A thank-you, for saving us," Henri explained.

James held up a shiny object. "Here," he said shyly.

Sarah took a look. James was holding a small home-made gold locket on a chain. It wasn't the fancy one her father had given her, but Sarah knew she would treasure this one every bit as much. "For me?" she asked with surprise as she took the locket in her hand and held it to her neck.

"Moses made it," James told her as he helped fasten the chain around her neck.

"It was my idea!" Henri announced proudly.

"It's beautiful," Sarah assured them.

"You like it?" James asked hopefully.

"I love it! But where in the world did you get the gold?" Sarah looked down at James's hands. His ring was gone.

"Are you sure you like it?" James asked again.

Sarah smiled warmly. "It's the greatest gift I've ever received."

September 1774

Dearest Mother,

So much has happened, I hardly know where to begin! Your latest letter brought the shocking news from London. It's terrible that Dr. Franklin has lost his position as postmaster, but praise the Lord he didn't end up in jail or worse! Please give my best to Dr. Franklin.

As he may have told you, Parliament's closing of Boston Harbor after the Boston Tea Party has not been warmly received. Representatives from all thirteen colonies are meeting here to draft a formal response to Parliament about the unfairness of closing the harbor.

The representatives call themselves the Continental Congress. This is the first time representatives from all the different colonies have gathered in one place to discuss their common problems.

There is so much beauty here. It is not difficult to understand why the people are passionate about their colonies. And passions, as you know, can make men's blood run hot.

Your loving daughter,
Sarah

# Chapter Thirteen

Winter passed into spring, and spring into summer. Throughout the year, Sarah, James, Henri, and Moses tried to keep some sense of normalcy in their lives. Moses and the boys spent their days publishing and distributing the *Gazette*, and Sarah continued reading, studying, and writing her letters home. But it wasn't easy staying normal—not when so many changes were going on in the colonies. And nowhere were the changes more obvious than in Philadelphia.

Ships were coming into the harbor almost daily. Some brought Red Coats, and some brought merchants from Europe. But the captains of all the ships had the same fears—that their sailors would be swept up in the passion of the colonists.

In September, a merchant ship pulled into the harbor. As the sailors went ashore, their captain had a stern warning for them. "Aw-right," he said in his strong cockney English accent. "These colonies 'r' troublin' with England in Boston. 'This is not Massachusetts,' y'all say. But trouble moves around. Leave your politics onboard. And don't pick up any politics ashore. Go on then, off with you."

Seventeen-year-old William Parker swung his bag over his shoulder and walked off the boat onto the dock. He'd never been to Philadelphia before. All around him were people walking, running, and selling their wares. It was an amazing city. He just had to draw it.

William sat down on the banks of the Delaware River and took a piece of charcoal and a pad from his bag. His hand moved quickly as he sketched the water, and the seagulls, the bridges and the ships in the harbor. From William's point of view, all was calm in Philadelphia.

But in truth, Philadelphia was not a calm place. In fact, the politics of revolution had made their way here. At that very moment, John Adams and his older cousin Sam were in Benjamin Franklin's print shop working on pamphlets that they hoped would fuel the fires that had already begun to burn in the hearts of the people of Boston.

"Sam, it's vital these pamphlets are distributed in Boston immediately," John insisted. "The pamphlets need to be read while the British warships are still there with cannons pointing at church steeples. It's an outrage we can exploit!"

Sam shook his head. Once again, his cousin had exaggerated the situation. "John," he said, "even I wouldn't accuse the British of targeting church steeples. And I consider myself an expert at stirring the pot."

"You're right, of course," John admitted with very little apology in his tone. "It's too much. But we must get these pamphlets into Boston. We must!"

Moses stood in the doorway. He smiled as he watched the two cousins' conversations. "You gentlemen have a way of agreeing that makes it sound like you're arguing," he teased.

John Adams laughed. "When Sam Adams is in top form, pigeons are shaken from their nests for three miles square."

"John, you sell me short," Sam countered, chuckling. "It's *five* miles square. And may I remind you, when you warm to a subject, you could talk the devil himself into a life of prayer."

Moses laughed. "Your pamphlets are nearly done," he assured the men as he led them into the room where Henri and James were finishing up the printing project.

"Sarah, Henri, James," Moses said as the men entered the room. "You remember Mr. Samuel Adams?"

James smiled brightly and let go of the arm of the printing machine. Henri was suddenly left holding the arm—and it was far too heavy for the little guy. As the arm moved upward, it dragged Henri up with it. He hung in the air with his feet dangling. He waved his legs wildly trying to move the arm back down.

James didn't notice Henri's troubles. He was too focused on speaking to Sam Adams. "We were there in Boston the night of the Tea Party."

"Were you?" Sam Adams answered. "Excellent. A most splendid protest. The people should never rise up without doing something worth remembering."

"And this is Mr. *John* Adams," Moses interrupted, introducing the kids to the other gentleman.

James's eyes lost their warmth and respect. Instead, he studied John Adams suspiciously. Everyone in the colonies knew about Sam Adams's younger cousin. He was a lawyer and a notorious one at that.

"Are you the same John Adams who defended the British troops who fired on our patriots at the Boston Massacre?"

"James, that was many years ago," Moses said quickly.

"No Moses, the lad is right," John Adams answered. "I did defend the British soldiers. And they were found *not* guilty for a good reason. They *weren't* guilty."

"And our patriots *were?*" James demanded. "They simply stood up for what they believed, just like at the Tea Party."

"I think it was very brave of you, Mr. Adams," Sarah stood up and walked over toward the men. "To defend unpopular men in the midst of friends and neighbors who wanted to see them punished. That took courage."

"I had justice on my side," John Adams reminded her. "The men involved in the so-called massacre were not patriots . . . They were a drunken mob, spoiling for a fight. It was a case of self defense." John looked over at James. "Facts can be stubborn things," he added.

"If I had been there, I would have been with the patriots," James insisted.

"Son, I admire your heart," John Adams said sincerely. "But you must learn to distinguish between a patriotic act of protest and mob rule. The tyranny of the people can be just as brutal as the tyranny of the crown."

Sam Adams was barely listening to his cousin's discussion with James. He was too busy checking over the printed sheets. "The pamphlet looks good, John," he interrupted. "Now all we need is a way to get them into Boston."

John Adams turned to the young patriot standing beside him. "How about you, James?" he said. "Here's a patriotic act. Get these to my wife, Abigail."

"There are wagons bound for Boston loading on the docks," Sam Adams added.

"I would," James assured the men. "But I've agreed to assist the scribes during the Congress."

"What about me?" Henri asked as he gave the print arm one more huge yank, and slowly lowered himself to the ground.

"What about you?" Moses asked with surprise.

"Since the harbor's closed, British troops patrol the roads, stopping and searching every carriage. There will be danger," Sam Adams explained to Henri.

"Abigail is going meet the convoy well outside

Boston," John Adams reminded his cousin. "The danger will be minimal."

Suddenly Sarah leaped to attention. "I'll go," she volunteered.

James was shocked. "You?" he asked incredulously. "You don't even believe in our cause."

"Maybe not," Sarah agreed. "But I believe in adventure. I could take Henri with me. No one would suspect a thing."

"Sarah is right," Moses agreed. "And Henri is a stout, able, young man. Right, Henri?"

As Henri opened his mouth to answer, he relaxed his pull on the heavy print arm. It shot up in the air, carrying Henri with it. The boy flew through the air and landed on the ground with a thud. After a moment, he struggled to his feet, and gave the Adams cousins a brave little salute.

"Good, it's settled," John Adams said. "I'll notify Abigail by courier."

# Chapter Fourteen

That night, James helped Sarah and Henri carry the pamphlets to the wagons that would soon be heading toward Boston. It was late, and only taverns were open as the trio walked down Chestnut Street. As they walked, Sarah and James were busy arguing over the discussion James had had with John Adams that afternoon. Henri kept himself happy sitting on top of the pamphlets as James wheeled the wheelbarrow through the streets. Henri liked when James gave him a ride.

"You have to learn to be aggressive if you want to be a reporter," James told Sarah.

"I think you were very nearly rude to Mr. Adams," Sarah countered.

"I was to the point," James insisted. "Nose to nose."

"You were as busy giving your own opinion as getting his."

"I like *Sam* Adams," James told her. "Sam is a man of action. This is a time for action."

Before Sarah could answer, a series of angry voices echoed out into the night from within one of the taverns.

This sounded like news! James stopped the wheelbarrow so suddenly that Henri went somersaulting out onto the street.

"Hey, wait a minute, you," one of the angry, drunken men slurred. "Stand right where you are."

William Parker, the sailor from the merchant ship docked in the harbor, tried to walk away. But a group of three men circled around him.

"I was looking for my shipmate," William told the crowd. "I'll be on my way."

"I offered to buy you a drink," one of the men insisted, his eyes glazed over with fury and alcohol.

"I don't drink," William said simply.

"That's it?" the man asked suspiciously. "Or is it you wouldn't join the toast? May Parliament rot, those wretched louts!"

"Let me go about my business," William insisted.

"You are my business," the angry man told William in a menacing tone. He looked toward the other colonists. "We'll teach you a song by our own John Dickinson."

And with that, the three men burst into song. " 'Then join hand in hand, brave Americans all! By uniting we stand, by dividing we fall.' "

As the drunken colonists belted out their song in powerful—if off-key—voices, James turned to walk toward the action. Sarah grabbed him before he could take even one step. "Where are you going?" she demanded. "I don't know my way at night."

James sighed. He obviously couldn't leave her to wander the streets of Philadelphia after dark. "Oh, all right, already," he moaned, listening as the mob grew angrier.

"I'm worried about you, out in the chilly night air," one of the men said. Of course he did not sound concerned about William Parker at all. He sounded mean and threatening. "He needs a warm coat of tar and feathers!"

Suddenly, the three men pounced on William. They grabbed the teen and carried him off through the dark, menacing streets of Philadelphia.

As the men's voices drifted off into the distance, James scowled at Sarah. "I can't believe I'm going to miss this," he grumbled.

"I can't believe you'd want to have anything to do with it. If you were a real gentleman, you'd put a stop to it."

"Imagine how silly he's going to look covered with tar and feathers. He'll look like a giant barn owl," James said, laughing. Then he folded his arms like wings and flapped them wildly. "Hooty hoot. I'm hooty the sailor."

Henri giggled, but Sarah was not amused. She continued walking toward the harbor. She had an adventure to begin.

★ ★ ★

The docks were a busy place that evening. Tons of rice and flour were being loaded onto cargo wagons. It took several men to lift the bags of food onto the wagons that would make up the caravan.

"Isn't this more of a story than that poor, unfortunate sailor?" Sarah asked James.

"What story?" James asked as he hoisted up a pile of pamphlets. "We're loading wagons."

Sarah shook her head in disbelief. Didn't this boy know anything? "These supplies have been sent from four different colonies. That's a story! I had the impression the colonies considered themselves separate countries."

James nodded. "They did, until Parliament closed Boston Harbor. If they can do it to Boston, they can do it anywhere." He smiled triumphantly. If Parliament had hoped to stop the revolution by punishing Boston, they had failed miserably. By closing the harbor, they'd succeeded only in uniting the colonists. But before he could tell Sarah just that, their discussion was interrupted by the laughter and shouts of an angry mob. James turned to see what was happening.

In the distance he saw a mob of more than ten drunken men parading through the streets. They carried a huge rail. Lying on the rail was a man completely covered from head to toe in black tar and a thousand feathers.

"What is it?" Henri asked, struggling to see.

"It's the barn owl on parade," James laughed. "Hooty hoot. Hooty hoot."

But William Parker didn't look like a barn owl at all. He looked like a scared seventeen-year-old who feared for his life. "Let me go," he cried out. "Leave me alone! What is my crime, that I disagree?"

James couldn't contain his excitement. "Now *that's* a story," he told Sarah. "I want to see what happens next!" And with that, he took off after the mob.

Henri tried to trail behind him, but Sarah grabbed the little Frenchman by the collar. "Hold on, Henri," she told him. "We're leaving soon. The wagon master said the roads out of Philadelphia are easier to travel with this moon."

Henri sighed. Sarah was right: They had a mission. He turned and waved good-bye to James. But James was too busy imitating a barn owl to wave back.

Sarah sighed. Life in the colonies was so confusing. Here she could see people loading up food to share with their fellow colonists. That gave her hope for mankind. But at that same time on that very same street, she could see grown men callously bullying a sailor not more than two years older than herself. And to make things worse, now James was caught up in it. It made Sarah wonder what was at the true heart of the colonies—compassion or cruelty?

Which would carry the day?

# Chapter Fifteen

The next morning, as Sarah and Henri journeyed to Boston, James found himself alone with Moses in the print shop. And he was determined to make the most of the situation.

With Dr. Franklin in London, a lot of the decisions about what would appear in the *Gazette* lay with Moses. James had to run his ideas past him if they were ever going to be printed. And at the moment he had a great idea for a story.

"In large type across the top, 'Hooty Hoot Gets the Boot,'" James suggested, using his hands to show how big the headline should be. "Because he looked like a barn owl after they tarred and feathered him. And they kicked him when they cut him loose! Get it? Hoot-Boot."

Moses shook his head disappointingly. "I don't think so."

James frowned. Didn't Moses understand? "He had it coming," James insisted.

But Moses wasn't convinced that William Parker had deserved what had happened to him. "Remember what John Adams said about mobs?" he asked James.

"What does Mr. Adams know about the newspaper game?" James said with a tone of superiority in his voice. "He could learn something from the author of that pamphlet he's sending to Boston. Novanglus. Now that man's a writer."

Moses laughed. "Novanglus *is* John Adams. It's a pseudonym, meaning he writes under an assumed name."

James was amazed. "John Adams wrote 'a government of laws not men'? That's John Adams?"

"It is."

James considered that for a moment. "Maybe I should write using a . . . a . . . a . . ." He struggled to recall the word.

"Pseudonym."

"Yeah. I'll call myself something modern," James thought aloud. "DaggerQuill. All one word but capitalize the Q."

Moses rolled his eyes. "ChatterQuill would be more like it. The lesson here, James, is less about the name and more about the message. Mr. Adams is a very wise man. You would do well to learn from his example. Now get that paper stock over to the Congress."

James scowled. "ChatterQuill," he mumbled. "Humph!"

Moses ignored James's muttering. "They're gathering at Carpenters' Hall," he told the teen.

James brightened a little. "Will you let me write a story about the Congress for the *Gazette*?"

"Only if you study the issue," Moses told him. "Learn about the men arguing the various sides."

"Deal!" James shouted as he raced out the door for Carpenters' Hall.

Moses sighed. James was so impulsive.

Within a second, the teen was back. "I forgot the paper stock," he said sheepishly as he grabbed the bundles and hurried off.

★ ★ ★

The Congress was already in session by the time James arrived at Carpenters' Hall. As he entered, he noticed John Adams and his cousin Sam on the porch of the building.

"I could choke half of them with my bare hands!" Sam exclaimed. "Don't they understand the suffering that's going on in Boston?"

"Patience, Sam," John urged. "We will make the case with the facts, stacked one upon another, like bricks. Soon we will have an argument so strong, it will be impervious to attack. We need every colony to support us, or Boston will be left to the mercy of Parliament."

As John and Sam entered the building, James did the same. He looked around for the best seat. He decided to sit near the back of the room, beside a scribe who was recording the minutes of the meeting. A well-dressed man with an accent that sounded slightly Southern got up to speak.

"Who is that?" James asked the scribe.

"Him? That's Patrick Henry," the scribe said of the delegate from Virginia.

James listened as Patrick spoke. It was hard not to get caught up in his speech. He was a dramatic speaker, who used the English language in a way James had never heard before.

As Patrick Henry addressed the delegates, many of

the men in the room chimed in and raised their arms. One man even rose to his feet during the speech.

"Who is that standing up?" James asked the scribe.

"Delegate Duane," the scribe whispered. "He's from New York."

James was quiet for a moment, watching as John Adams waved his quill pen like a flag, trying to get the attention of the members of the Congress.

"I second the motion to recognize Mr. Randolph as the president of the very first Continental Congress," John Adams declared, throwing his support solidly behind representative Peyton Randolph of Virginia.

"That's John Adams. Him I know," James told the scribe. "Let's make a deal. I'll tell you everyone I know, and you tell me everyone you know."

That didn't seem like much of a deal to the scribe. "I know everyone," he told James in a voice that didn't hide his irritation.

"Everyone?" James asked doubtfully. He pointed to a man who'd recently risen from his chair.

"John Jay of New York," the scribe said, sighing. "Now please, I'm trying to listen."

"As we set about our business, I remind everyone of our purpose," John Jay remarked. "We are here to reestablish harmony with Great Britain. We are not here to provoke Parliament into further action against us."

Patrick Henry addressing Congress

James listened intently. Another man rose and gave his opinion. "In the same breath, we should—I beseech you—examine the merits of the dispute with the Mother Country and take such steps as will reunite us firmly as one people."

James frowned. He, himself, had no desire to reunite with the British. The teen was all for revolution. "Who's that?" James asked, barely hiding the disgust in his voice.

"Galloway. From Pennsylvania. He's our colony's delegate." The scribe looked straight at James. "Any chance you'd sit by the other scribe?" he asked hopefully. "He has a better view, and he's deaf in one ear."

"Okay, I get the hint," James agreed.

"It wasn't a hint," the scribe assured him.

Before James could move his seat, however, John Adams held up his hand. As soon as he was called on, he sprang to his feet. "I have just received a message by courier that British warships have fired cannons upon the city of Boston," he announced.

A hush came over the room as the men waited eagerly for John Adams to continue.

"Church steeples have fallen!" John exclaimed, knowing full well that he was greatly exaggerating. But he was determined to change the course of this conversation—no matter what he had to say or do. He had to convince the other members of the Congress to help the people of Massachusetts in their struggle. "There is panic in the streets . . . And some number . . . of dead," he added.

A feeling of excitement—of history in the making—ran through James's body. Surely now, the colonies would take action.

September 1774

Dearest Mother,

This land is even more spectacular than Father has described in his letters. But the people I have met are most uncommon. Their desire to learn what is going on with their fellow colonials gives me hope for mankind.

On our second day, an old man brought his sheep to the convoy. He explained he was too old to continue herding sheep. He had given most of his flock to his daughter, but he wanted to give the rest to the blockaded city of Boston. At first, our wagon master didn't want to accept the flock. But I had an idea: Henri loves games, and what better way to keep him occupied than to put him in charge of an army of sheep, and give him a collie as his second in command.

Everywhere along the road there are people with news and questions, and rumors take wing! I understand now what Dr. Franklin said about the value of pamphlets and newspapers. It's harder for rumors to spread when the facts are there in black and white.

Your loving daughter,
Sarah

# Chapter Sixteen

Sarah had plenty of time to admire the beauty of America. She knew that the trip from Philadelphia to Boston by land was long and tedious. Even under the best of conditions it could take more than six days, much of it over dirt roads and mud. Sarah spent much of the time laughing as Henri took charge of his sheep. He called the animals his "troops." And with the help of a trusty collie, whom he'd named Lieutenant, General Henri was able to keep the sheep in line as the convoy made its way to Boston. Sarah was just glad it kept him occupied through the long, tedious journey.

Sarah's travels did eventually come to an end. After so many days on the road, the convoy was finally met by a carriage. As the driver brought the carriage to a stop, Sarah could see a beautiful woman in the seat beside him. She seemed so poised and controlled. Witout ever being introduced, Sarah knew that this must be Abigail Adams. She matched her husband's description perfectly.

"Welcome from all the good people of Boston," Abigail greeted the weary travelers. "Welcome and thank you."

As Abigail got down from her perch at the front of the carriage, Henri led his "troops" over toward her. He had successfully completed his mission.

"Lieutenant, we have a meeting at headquarters," the boy told the collie as he continued with his game. "Move the squad, Lieutenant."

The dog did as he was told. He barked loudly and herded the sheep toward the wagon.

"You must be Sarah," Abigail said, greeting the teenage girl. "Forgive my brazen husband, that Mr. Adams, for sending a young woman on such an errand. He will hear from me."

Sarah smiled. "Thank him for me. It's been a wonderful adventure. But I must ask you, we heard that Boston has been fired upon! Is this true?"

Abigail looked at her curiously. "Heavens, no! General Gage sent troops to Cambridge and took arms and powder stored there. Patrols on the road stop supplies from entering the city. But actual warfare, heavens no!"

Sarah smiled with relief. She'd been so worried. "Has any word come from England?" she asked. "Anything new from Parliament that might provoke violence?"

Abigail shook her head. "No. General Gage can act under his own authority. He claims he seized the powder and guns to prevent violence." She glanced at the pile of papers Sarah had brought with her. "However, if he finds these pamphlets, that would be sedition. That could land us all in jail."

Henri walked up to Abigail just as she mentioned jail. "Sedition?"he asked curiously.

"That's like treason," Sarah explained.

Abigail gave the children a warm, reassuring smile. "You have nothing to fear," she assured them both. "I won't let anything happen to you. My promise."

Sarah smiled back at Abigail. After so many months surrounded by nothing but men and boys, it was nice to hear a woman's tender voice.

"I know how to get the pamphlets into Boston without anyone going to jail," Henri suddenly piped up He pointed to his sheep. "My squadron."

Sarah scowled at him. "Henri! This is not a game!"

Henri shook his head. He knew that. He was perfectly serious. "We can make saddlebags covered in wool. Each of my soldiers can carry two bundles. If I follow the marsh road into Boston, no one will think twice."

Abigail eyes danced brightly. "Young man, that's brilliant."

Sarah couldn't have agreed more. "It *is* brilliant," she agreed, unable to hide the amazement in her voice. "How in the world did you come up with it?"

Henri shrugged. "Just like Hannibal crossed the Alps with his elli-phants," he explained, recalling the story of how the Carthaginian general Hannibal had led his troops across the Alps on elephants and attacked Rome way back in 218 B.C. "Dr. Franklin told me all about it." Henri stood tall, striking a military pose.

Sarah laughed. What a good thing that this little general had learned his lessons so well.

✫ ✫ ✫

As Henri spent the evening uniforming his four-legged soldiers with saddlebags filled with pamphlets, James was busy in Philadelphia, venting his frustration with the Congress to Moses.

"I found the delegates at Carpenters' Hall arguing

over what to do about the Intolerable Acts," he told Moses. "It comes down to this. One group wants to demand Parliament repeal the Intolerable Acts, while the other group want to ask the king for his help. You know, get him to make Parliament change its mind."

Moses thought about that. "Who's saying what?" he asked pointedly. "Who are the leaders?"

"The firebrands," James explained. "That's what the moderates called them. They're the Massachusetts men—John Adams and Sam Adams."

Moses nodded. "Write the names down," he instructed.

James dipped his quill in the inkwell and did as Moses suggested.

"Who are the moderates, then?" Moses continued. "Who speaks for them?"

James scowled. "Our own delegation, can you believe it? Shame on Pennsylvania! Mr. Galloway sounds as if he were a member of Parliament himself! Then there are Duane and Jay from New York. They're the most vocal."

Moses smiled proudly. "Good job, James," he praised him. "Excellent reporting. You have all the facts." Moses had expected James to beam at such praise. But instead, the teen looked defeated. "Why are you so glum?" he asked.

"Because they just talk and talk and talk," James said, his voice brimming with frustration. "Why won't they fight it out and be done with it?"

"Let's say a prayer of thanks we have men who aren't so quick to fight," Moses said with the wisdom of a man who had seen too much fighting already. "Battles are easy to start; they aren't so easy to stop."

"The moderates won," James assured Moses. "They're going to petition the king to fix it with Parliament. It could be *weeks* before there's any news. Moses, let me do a story on the sailor who got tarred and feathered. That's real news. Patriotic and funny!"

Moses looked seriously at James. He didn't seem to view the story of the sailor as quite so brave . . . or humorous. "I know where you can find the sailor," he told the teen. "Maybe you should talk to him and see how 'patriotic and funny' it is."

A look of excitement came over James. He couldn't wait to get started on the story.

He didn't have to wait long. That evening, Moses brought James to the office of the local doctor who had treated William Parker after the tar and feathering. "You want to ask Mr. Parker questions for the news-paper?" he doctor asked James.

"Yes, doctor," James began. He stopped as he heard

a loud cry come from the next room. The crying was followed by an agonizing moan.

"He's in a great deal of pain," the doctor explained to James. "He'll have to stay in bed for a month, maybe more."

That news surprised James. "He's hurt bad?" he asked. "He can't be. I saw him. I saw him stand up and walk away."

William Parker moaned again, as if to answer James himself. "When a person is tarred, the tar is like hot oil," the doctor explained. "They boil it. They pour it over the victim's head. Tar burns a man's clothes onto his skin—"

"You mean like hot candle wax," James interrupted. "And you peel it off and—"

"Worse!" the doctor assured James. "When you peel tar off, you peel the skin away. Then there is the risk of infection, which I'm afraid has already set in."

James was confused. He'd been so certain that this had all been a harmless protest . . . but now he wasn't so sure. "But they were Patriots," he thought aloud. "Taking a stand—"

"They were criminals," the doctor told James in no uncertain terms, "who robbed him of his hard-earned pay."

"But they were shouting slogans against Parliament, and they sang a liberty song," James said, his voice sounding suddenly unsure.

"Did they respect Mr. Parker's liberty?" the doctor asked.

James had no answer for that.

"You want the real story? Go ask him a question," the doctor suggested. "Go on."

Suddenly James felt very young and frightened. "I don't think I want to . . ."

"The facts, James," Moses reminded him. "If you want to be a reporter, you must have all the facts."

James understood. The only thing he'd ever wanted to be was a reporter. And no one had ever promised him it would be easy. He took a deep breath and slowly followed Moses and the doctor into William Parker's small hospital room.

The room was softly lit by only a few candles, so as not to hurt William's eyes. There wasn't much furniture—just a medical table, and a wrought-iron bed, where William Parker lay moaning and crying in pain.

It took a while for James to move closer. As he walked toward the bed he could see what the tar had done. There were bandages over most of William Parker's body and at least half his face. It was obvious that even after his burns had healed, William would carry the scars of that night all over his body for the rest of his life. The pain seemed almost unbearable. The young sailor alternated between crying and screaming out in pain.

"Tears are salty," Moses explained to James. "That adds sting to the wounds. One tear leads to more hurt and more tears. It's a cycle of pain no man should inflict on another for any reason."

"Who is it?" William Parker cried out. His wounds had left him unable to turn his head and see who had entered his room.

"It's Moses. I brought the young man I mentioned earlier. Could he ask you a question or two?"

"Yes," William replied weakly.

James could feel the tears welling up in his eyes. William Parker wasn't much older than he was. That made it even harder for James to see him in such pain. Suddenly the tarring and feathering didn't seem like an act of bravery and patriotism. It seemed cruel and cowardly. "Is . . . there . . . any-thing . . . I can do?" James asked the injured man.

Moses looked down at James with pride and placed his hand on his shoulder for support. The new reporter had learned a hard lesson. But he had learned it well.

★　　　★　　　★

# Chapter Seventeen

Sarah reached for a slice of bread and tried not to be nervous. She and the other members of the convoy were having dinner in a field just outside of Boston. They'd put planks of wood together to form a table, and had set up a meal of vegetables, fruit, meat, and potatoes.

Everyone Sarah had traveled with was there, other than Henri. He had gone off with Abigail Adams's driver to sneak the pamphlets into Boston.

Sarah watched Abigail carefully. The woman seemed calm and in control. Sarah wished she could be more like her, but she was so worried about Henri that she could barely eat.

Sarah's fears worsened when four Red Coats suddenly arrived at the farmhouse. Without even so much as a greeting, they walked over to the wagons and began to lift the tarps that covered the cargo.

"These wagons headed toward Boston?" one of the British soldiers asked.

No one said a word.

"Somebody got an answer for me?" he demanded.

"Yes, they are," Sarah answered finally, trying to keep her voice from shaking. "They were loaded in accordance with the law of the king and were documented."

The soldier looked at Sarah curiously. "By the sound of that voice, you're a ways from home here, missy."

Sarah frowned. This soldier had a British accent, just as she did. But he wasn't acting at all like the English gentlemen Sarah was used to. None of the soldiers were. The Red Coats were holding their muskets at the ready. And if Sarah wasn't mistaken, she'd heard two of them whispering about how they should take the wagons themselves. They were considering selling the goods the colonists had sent to Boston, and pocketing the money themselves. Sarah was not about to let that happen!

"Sir, my father is a British officer," she informed one of the Red Coats. "I believe we should discuss your behavior."

That caught the men off guard. "Really?" one of them asked nervously. "An officer, you say?"

Abigail Adams stepped forward, holding a scroll of paper in her hand. "Which of you would like to sign for the wagons?" she asked, almost daring the men to go ahead with their plan. "I'm sure General Gage will want to know who took the supplies."

At the sound of the general's name, the Red Coats suddenly lost all of their braveness.

"General Gage?" one asked, his voice scaling up with panic. "See, we didn't know these goods were . . ." He stared at Sarah with surprise. "She's not the daughter of . . . ?"

"We don't need to make an issue of who her father is," Abigail said, her voice brimming with authority. "Just sign."

"We don't have time to take the wagons now," one of the Red Coats said quickly. He glanced at the wagons. "There aren't any newspapers or pamphlets here?"

Sarah smiled. "I swear on the king's health. There are no printed or published works in these wagons."

The Red Coats were sweating now. "Move on, then," one of the soldiers ordered as he followed his fellow soldiers down the road.

Abigail smiled at Sarah. She reached over and gave her a huge hug. Sarah's quick thinking had saved the day.

✷ ✷ ✷

Sarah hadn't lied to the Red Coats. There were no printed or published works in the wagons. They were all with Henri and his army of sheep. And at that very moment, Henri, along with Abigail's driver, was approaching the marshes outside of Boston—a favorite hiding place of a patrol of Red Coats.

"All right, get down," one of the soldiers ordered as he ducked down behind some tall reeds and grasses. He listened as Henri's footsteps grew closer. "Stay quiet until we know what we're up against."

The Red Coats huddled together as Henri and his sheep squadron approached. The soldiers couldn't see beyond the reeds and grass. But they *could* hear what seemed like a huge patrol of soldiers approaching the marsh. After all, each sheep was walking on four feet. One sheep sounded like two men to the hidden Red Coats.

Henri was completely unaware that he was surrounded by Red Coats. He was too busy playing his army game to think of that. "Colonel, have we heard from the Indian scouts?" he asked in a deep, authoritative voice. "They are the famous Shadow Warriors.

You can't see them until they're right beside you."

One of the British soldiers tried to peer over the reeds, to see what they were up against. One of the others pulled him down. "Are you trying to get us killed?" he demanded in a loud whisper.

"They sound like sheep," his fellow soldier whispered back.

"It could be Indians. They make noises like birds and bears to fool the enemy," another soldier suggested. "They must have taught the rebels how to do it. Let's get out of here!"

The British soldiers took off like frightened rabbits. That left the roadway clear for Henri and his army to complete their mission.

✯ ✯ ✯

Sarah was relieved when Henri and the driver returned to the convoy. She was very proud of the brave French boy. She was also sad that the mission was over. It was time to go back to Philadelphia. Sarah knew she was going to miss Abigail Adams dreadfully. She also knew she would never forget her. All her life, Sarah would strive to be like the brave and considerate Mrs. Adams.

Henri was sad to say his good-byes as well. He'd become very attached to the collie who'd helped him control his army. But it was time to return the dog to his rightful owner—the old man who'd so generously donated the sheep to the people of Boston. That man had no idea just how important those sheep had been to their mission.

John Adams was thrilled to greet Sarah and Henri as their wagon arrived in Philadelphia. The firebrand had been concerned that the mission could become dangerous. But seeing the children safe and sound, and knowing that they had spent time with his wife, Abigail, brought him a sense of calm.

Sarah handed Mr. Adams a letter from his wife. She watched as the usually forceful man's face softened. "Thank you so much," John Adams said. "I worry about her out there in harm's way with our sweet children."

"She asks you to write more often," Sarah told him.

The statesman nodded. "Yes. I must." He smiled at Sarah. "If you would include a message for Dr. Franklin in your next letter to England, tell him I am as heartstrong as headstrong. I am convinced by this Congress that America will support Massachusetts or perish with her."

"I will tell him that," she assured him.

As a show of gratitude for their bravery, John Adams invited James, Henri, Sarah, and Moses to see the Congress in action. Although they weren't allowed to sit in the gallery, they could watch the goings-on from a spot near the side doorway of Carpenters' Hall.

"The distinctions between Virginians, Pennsylvanians, New Yorkers, and New Englanders are obsolete," John Adams said in an address to his fellow congressmen. "I am not a New England man. I am an American."

James smiled and looked over at Henri and Sarah. "That's what this Congress has really been about," he whispered. "It's about all of us realizing something important: *We are Americans.*"

It was true. When the British put a blockade on Boston Harbor, everything changed. The colonies were now united as one.

Nothing would ever be the same.

# The Pennsylvania Gazette

## FRANKLIN PLEDGES TO PAY FOR TEA!

by James Hiller
Philadelphia, 1773

Benjamin Franklin has announced that he will personally pay for the tea destroyed during the Boston Tea Party—if Parliament would agree to repeal the tea tax in the colonies. Franklin vowed to turn over his entire fortune to cover the expenses brought to the East India Company, whose tea was onboard the "Dartmouth" during the raid.

Dr. Franklin has been in London, negotiating with Parliament on behalf of the colonists. He has had some success in the recent past. His speeches and negotiations against the Stamp Act are considered largely responsible for the Stamp Act being repealed.

However, sources say that the British are unlikely to end the tea tax, despite Dr. Franklin's generous offer. It appears Dr. Franklin's usefulness in Europe is coming to an end. He may return to the colonies soon.

# THOMAS PAINE STOKES THE FIRES OF REVOLUTION

by James Hiller
Philadelphia, 1774

Mr. Thomas Paine has made his way from England to the colonies. Mr. Paine has arrived on our shores with a letter of recommendation from Benjamin Franklin, and has agreed to become a contributing editor to the "Philadelphia Magazine."

Mr. Paine did not have an easy journey. He caught fever onboard and had to be carried to our shores. But his arrival is already being heralded by many of the firebrands in the Congress.

The firebrands, led by Samuel Adams, John Adams, and Patrick Henry, represent those members of our colonial society who favor breaking with England. They were given the nickname firebrands because, like a stick of wood with a spark of fire on its end, these men are lighting a revolutionary fire in the hearts and minds of our people. The firebrands are in conflict with more moderate members of the Congress such as John Jay of New York, and our own Mr. Galloway of Pennsylvania. They would prefer to find a way to remain part of the British Empire if it is at all possible.

When asked how it felt to become involved in colonial politics so soon after arriving on our shores, Mr. Paine wrote, "I thought it very hard to have the country set on fire . . . almost the moment I got into it."

Spoken as a true firebrand.

Sarah Phillips

James Hiller

Moses

Benjamin Franklin

John Adams

Henri Lefebvre